SHADOWS AND SINS

The body of a woman has been discovered in Castle Farthing Woods, and it appears that although she had been dead for years, nobody had ever reported her missing. DI Harry Falconer of the Market Darley police is perplexed – and not only in his working life. He has recently resumed his relationship with psychologist, Dr Honey Dubois – but while visiting a local village in the course of his investigations, unsettling memories of a former love are revived. Then the bodies start to come thick and fast...

SHADOWS AND SINS

by

Andrea Frazer

Magna Large Print Books
Long Preston, North Yorkshire,
BD23 4ND, England.

British Library Cataloguing in Publication Data.

A catalogue record of this book is
available from the British Library

ISBN   978-0-7505-4485-6

First published in Great Britain by Accent Press 2016

Magna Large Print is an imprint of Library Magna Books Ltd.

Printed and bound in Great Britain by
T.J. (International) Ltd., Cornwall, PL28 8RW

For Tony and Belinda, who always come to my aid in times of need, and Greg, who knows what he does is good.

Chapter One

Early 2012

Christmas had come and gone, as had the enforced jollity of New Year and now, in late January, the countryside seemed to be wrapped in the dark hoar-cloak that was this time of year. Although the nights were, in reality, shortening, the impression was that on some days the sun barely cleared the horizon, and the landscape was almost in a constant state of frozen darkness.

'Davey' Carmichael, a detective sergeant with the CID in the small town of Market Darley, and who lived in the nearby village of Castle Farthing, had taken to walking his dogs very early in the morning, in the woods near his home. At this time of year, the dead bracken and the bare trees, either studded with frost or dripping a melancholy rhythm of cold water, seemed to match his mood.

Since the mid-winter celebrations of the previous month, the ultimate collector had paid a visit to the Market Darley police force with his scythe and hourglass, and made away with one of their own. It was unthinkable; not only because of the circumstances under which the passing had happened but also because it was someone young, with his whole future ahead of him.

Carmichael was only too well aware that he had almost been called himself, after a grave injury suffered while on duty the previous year, and he felt sobered and diminished by recent events. It could so easily have been him. His household was a particularly warm and cheery one full of life, and his wife's body was bursting with new fruitfulness, as they had twins due later in the year – he couldn't bear the thought of being parted from them.

The dogs snuffled around the scent-laden ground, tracking trails of other, long-gone creatures and local friends, occasionally pausing to add their own marks and messages to the territory, as their owner paused to reflect once more on recent events.

How would they all manage with the loss of an officer – a friend – so integral to all their working lives? The initial news of what had happened had been like a practical joke in bad taste. That this dedicated officer could have risked so much in his professional life, only to pass into the next in such a quiet, nondescript way, was as unexpected as it had at first seemed impossible. His absence was keenly felt and, for those who had worked with him, particularly hard to bear.

PC Merv Green had not perished in a car accident, a violent attack by yobs, or as a result of any serious crime. He had not died on the job doing his duty as an officer of the law nor protecting the public. He had merely failed to turn up for his shift one morning and his fiancée, fellow officer PC Linda 'Twinkle' Starr, had gone round to his flat in her lunch break when he failed to answer either his landline or his mobile phone. She had expected him to have quarantined himself to bed with a heavy cold or influenza, and just forgotten to phone in. At worst, she thought he might have had a fall and might not be able to get to a phone. What she had found there had destroyed her hopes and dreams, and all their plans for their future together.

She had found Green still in his bed. Too still. His body was pale, his skin as cold as marble, and she realised that the man she sought was not really there at all, not in spirit; that he had gone off on what has sometimes been described as the greatest adventure ever, but which was in fact the end of her life as well as his, at that moment. He was dead, had passed away some time during the night, as he slept, perhaps dreaming of the new day and all that it would never bring.

Dr Christmas, Market Darley's Force Medical Examiner, had attended, and later carried out the post-mortem. It became apparent that PC Green had died from Sudden Adult Death Syndrome, and that there had been no way it could have been foretold, prevented or treated. It was just one of those filthy tricks that life sometimes plays when things seem to be going well.

This made the news no better, though, and the station was under a pall of gloom. Officers shuffled round without their usual optimism and hope that they would win the war against crime. PC Green had done a lot of work with CID, and his loss was felt well beyond the uniformed branch of the service. His fiancée, meanwhile, had been missing from work since finding his body. Her absence was as much of a reminder of his late status as his.

Claustrophobic, depressive January had certainly pulled no punches this year, and it had got off to a terrible start with the grim news of Green's death. The whole station, shocked beyond belief, had gone into collective mourning. Where once every corridor and office had thronged with life and enthusiasm, staff now shuffled from room to room, their gazes downcast, their mood introspective.

Superintendent Chivers, in an unusually human gesture, had permitted the wearing of black armbands for the week of the funeral, which had taken place the day before, and merry quips were even off the menu in the canteen. The sobriety of the atmosphere in the station was an ironic contrast to the cheery colours of the flowers, sent in tribute to the station and displayed throughout the public areas of the building in Green's memory.

Twinkle Starr had gone straight from the funeral to her parents' house in the north of England, having dragooned a friend to collect all her personal possessions from her locker, and had already applied for a transfer, to be taken up after a suitable period of compassionate leave. She had decided that she would keep in touch with no one, as she felt she would never recover, and wanted to wipe all memories of the couple's happy time together from her mind. She needed to reset the clock of her life and start from ground zero. It was unbearable for her to think now of the future she and Merv had planned together.

So every morning, DS Carmichael – particularly affected by the loss of PC Green, because of the man's similar age to his own and because he, Carmichael, had had few personal rather than professional dealings with death – woke in the gloom of the month's early hours. He put the dogs on their leads, and headed out into the misty chill of the dead woods where the surroundings matched his mood.

There were other early morning dog walkers and solitary wanderers to be found occasionally in the woods around the village of Castle Farthing. Carmichael would usually have waved, and called a cheery greeting to each person he passed, but recently this was not in his mood-span. He would merely give the briefest of nods and keep his eyes cast down in retrospection. There was a hole in his life where his colleague had been, and he did not comprehend how to fill it at the moment.

He was surprised by how shaken events had left him, as he dealt on a regular basis with the deaths of strangers and had felt himself a little inured to it. Even his immediate superior, Detective Inspector Harry Falconer, had become more morose and gloomy than usual. Never one of life's ebullient people – unlike Green, who had been full of joie de vivre – Falconer's serious and phlegmatic outlook on life had sunk almost into a miasma of gloom. There was little communication between them in their shared office, and most tasks were carried out with the minimum of conversation. The other officer who worked with them and who had not known Green well, felt excluded; not part of the club that constant professional contact with the deceased had engendered.

Giving a decisive tug on the dogs' leads, Carmichael headed back to the metalled road that would take him home for breakfast, before facing another day in what felt like an undertaker's establishment. In his less gloomy moments he did have the sensitivity to feel sorry for DC Tomlinson, who had not been there long enough to be part of 'the gang', but he didn't spend a lot of time on this. His own sense of loss was too strong. How could a man so full of life, as Merv had been, suddenly not be there anymore? How could he just *die?*

The sergeant's wife, Kerry, greeted him cheerily as she knew he needed all the encouragement she could offer to attempt to return his usually so sunny disposition to her. His adopted sons and year-old daughter greeted his return with equal enthusiasm, and the cheery glow of the log fire and the brightness of the lights soon improved his mood a tiny chink. Life was still good, he thought, noting his wife's expanding figure as she coped with carrying their twins and looking after their already-existing family. He just needed to get back in touch with the good things he knew he possessed in life.

There was nothing to be gained in indulging in 'what ifs'. No amount of longing would change what had happened. He just needed to accept it and move on, and not let the past scar his present, for he would never get this time of waiting and expectation back.

DI Harry Falconer had to drag himself out of bed these days. He thought he was immune to just about everything life could throw at him, given his years in the army and the police force, but this untimely death, so close to home, had left him floundering. He had been a fairly regular church attendee throughout his professional past, and always thought he had some sort of organic faith, but that had evaporated since the dreadful news of PC Green's death had hit the station.

His life was generally solitary; his on/off relationship with Heather Antrobus having fizzled out and his only regular company his five cats, but he felt himself more in need of the comfort of human contact these days. He had recently renewed his association with Dr Honey Dubois, an old flame who was now providing some much-needed warmth in his life.

With the ghost of a smile he remembered when she had first come to his home and encountered the cats. How could he be expected to understand that she had an innate horror of felines? Her resultant hysterics had appalled him. But when they had met again, she explained to him that she was determined to beat her phobia. She had been working with a colleague and volunteering at the local RSPCA centre in her free time, and now felt much more comfortable in the company of the furry creatures.

He was, at times, anxious about the importance of these occasional meetings. DI Falconer saw this as a weakness in himself, although he would eventually recognise it as a smattering of emotional maturity, even though he was finding it almost impossible to come to terms with how their relationship had soured the first time round. She at least offered him someone to bounce his feelings off, and he sorely needed that at the moment.

He had physical symptoms of his grief and confusion, had lost weight due to the decrease in his appetite, and traipsed round the station with the air of a lost child, not knowing quite where to go for guidance or aid. Even Bob Bryant, the irreplaceable and irrepressible desk sergeant, had lost a lot of his banter and bonhomie and looked across the reception desk with an unaccustomed dour countenance.

The run-up to this sad time had been the usual trivia of policing over the Christmas and New Year period – mainly opportunistic break-ins, drunken affrays and domestic violence. There was no big case consuming everyone's thoughts and actions, and therefore there was time to brood. If there was ever a time for a big case to break that time was fast arriving; even if only as a distraction and healing agent.

Falconer had taken to arriving at his office at an unheard-of early time. Not having the distraction of a wife, children, or dogs to walk, he would scuffle indolently through recent case histories, at sea as to what he could usefully apply himself to, in these doldrum days post-mortem.

That he had lost a lively, funny and enthusiastic member of his team, he was well aware, and the loss was doubly hard with the departure of Green's erstwhile fiancée, Twinkle. They had been a good double act, and would have made a fine fist of being married and raising a family. What a black joke life had indeed played. Considering what Twinkle had been through recently, sometimes he felt glad that he wasn't that close to anyone yet and therefore didn't have to face the destruction of his future through someone else's demise.

Listlessly riffling through his desk drawers in search of distraction, he settled down to await Carmichael's arrival and, maybe, the ringing of the telephone. He felt in desperate need for something to get his teeth into, although he would regret this wish later. He had always been told to be careful what he wished for, for he just might get it.

His restless and mainly pointless reverie was interrupted as a figure entered the office. It was the six-and-a-half-feet of Carmichael; considerably broadened in build since the beginning of their partnership a few years ago, when his huge hands and feet made a giant scarecrow of his silhouette. He was not much like this at the moment, as he wore an impossibly long black coat, black leather gloves, and a similarly midnight-like fedora hat. He was a nightmare on legs: Detective Sergeant Freddy Krueger. The Elm Street figure's jaws were moving rhythmically, but the inspector didn't have the heart to ask him to dispose of his bubble gum. Anything that gave him pleasure was OK at the moment.

Falconer barely nodded at him, having been confronted by this grim apparition since they had lost their colleague, and was now so used to it, he would have been surprised if his sergeant had turned up in normal garb – not that Carmichael had ever subscribed to what the world in general considered to be everyday clothing. The sergeant mumbled a greeting, shed his sinister outer garments, and slumped down behind his desk to begin listlessly looking through his emails.

17

'How's things?' murmured Falconer.

'A'right,' replied his sergeant.

'Kids?'

'A'right.'

'Kerry?'

'A'right.' Good Lord, he was low. Even his computer screen had a little black drape round its edges.

'How're the cats, sir?'

'All right.' He was similarly in low spirits.

And that's how things were. Morale in Market Darley Police Station was at an all-time low: a nadir it had not previously reached in his occupancy there.

Chapter Two

Seven o'clock the next morning found Carmichael back in the woods, his dogs snuffling around as had become their habit recently. They relished being given this glorious opportunity to communicate with other dogs and pick up their pee-mails. The owner's mind was miles away, remembering his lost colleague and assessing how he should be grateful that he was still living and breathing after his experience the year before. He had never fully recovered mentally from his brush with death and, at times, was very glad to still be alive, at others, depressed by how close he'd come to losing his life, and how easy it was to cease existing.

Shaking his head to fling off the mental fog, like

a dog emerging from water, and realising that it was now time for him to head back to Jasmine Cottage and his breakfast, he looked around, to find that the dogs had disappeared out of his view, which was very unusual. He gave a low whistle, then stilled to listen for the sound of them among the dripping trees. It was unusual for him to be so distracted that he actually lost physical sight of them.

After about thirty seconds he became aware of a slight scuffling away to his right behind a clump of withered bracken, and a little whine of excitement broke on the chilly air. What were the little devils up to? He wasn't in the mood for any of the usual games, and he headed towards where he had heard the sound.

'*Little* devils' wasn't exactly an accurate way of describing his pets, as their builds were disparate: although one was very low to the ground, the other was gigantic. Dipsy Daxie the dachshund had originally been the property of a suspect from a previous case, and Carmichael had adopted him when his owner no longer had the liberty to do so.

Mulligan was a Great Dane who had previously belonged to some neighbours. The Carmichaels had looked after him on several occasions when their neighbours had gone away, but the beast had grown to such enormous proportions that his former owners, being advanced in age, were unable to cope with him anymore.

Over the recent festivities, they had asked Carmichael if he would be willing to take on this monstrous beast. They were going to their daughter's for Christmas. She refused, point-blank, to have the creature in her home because of his sheer size – and had thought of the sergeant, as man and dog had always got on well together in the past. Carmichael was severely tempted, but somewhat concerned as he already had three dogs. A bit of thinking and bartering, however, produced the solution. The neighbours would take his little Yorkie and Chihuahua, Mr Knuckles and Mistress Fang, in exchange for the hulking thing the size of a small horse, with the proviso that Carmichael's adopted sons could take the small creatures for walks whenever they wanted to.

It was something that had been discussed at length in the Carmichael household before any action was taken. Kerry Carmichael had agreed: as much as she loved the little dogs, they were not ideal pets for her at that moment in time – tripping over them at that stage of her pregnancy was not an option.

Carmichael could visit his one-time dogs whenever he wanted, as could Mulligan's former owners visit their almost-horse. With Kerry as heavily pregnant as she was, the little dogs had got under her feet; God forbid that she should fall and harm either herself or the twins. The older boys had rather lost their interest in such little pets and so were much less concerned than they would have been a year ago: Mulligan was much more fun for a bit of rough and tumble.

Carmichael had not broken this news to Falconer yet. Mulligan regarded the inspector as one of his very best friends; whereas Falconer regarded Mulligan as a danger to humankind in general, and himself in particular.

20

Clearing his mind, Carmichael's heart lifted as he thought of the antenatal appointment to come and the fact that he would hear his babies' heartbeats, real and reassuring of the new lives to come. And the rest of the day was his to do what he wanted.

Into the office early as had now become habitual, Falconer sat at his desk looking unseeingly at his computer screen. When a call came in for someone to attend to a post-New Year break-in, he sent DC Tomlinson, who was glad to get outside where everything was not so focused on their departed colleague.

Before the DC returned, however, the inspector realised how confined he had felt recently, and was reminded that there were three bodies in the mortuary awaiting postmortem. They had died in a car crash, but Philip Christmas, the force's FME, had been away for a couple of days, visiting nephews and nieces. He would be back this morning, and the inspector grabbed his car keys and coat, and left the building with a feeling of relief. It may be a visit to more death, but at least he didn't know these people, had never laughed and joked with them about work.

Doc Christmas had not yet started his triple grisly task, and made a pot of Blue Mountain coffee for himself and Falconer to share before he got 'stuck in', as he phrased it, to his tasks.

'Scalpels at the ready, I suppose,' commented Falconer.

'Don't forget those delving hands of mine. I never know what they're going to turn up.'

21

'How you can be so light-hearted about this business I can't understand.'

'How else would I handle it, having to do it so often?'

'Don't know, but I'm glad I haven't got Carmichael with me. You know how he reacts to your slicing and dicing your victims.'

'Like a maiden aunt being flashed at by a pervert hung like a donkey. Now, to be serious, are you seeing that young lady of yours again? That psychiatrist you were going out with, and then dropped for no good reason I could discern.'

Falconer didn't enlighten him as to his reasoning, but his face broke into a small smile as he remembered he was having dinner with Honey that night. 'We're having a meal together later,' he volunteered. They had not met very frequently since their reunion, for he wanted their time together to be quality time, and not wasted in the company of others. It was important to him to test out this tentative renewal of the relationship, and he wanted to be sure of his feelings before he committed to any more time spent together.

Doc Christmas smiled back in approval and asked, 'Which restaurant?'

'Actually, it's not in a restaurant. It's at her place.'

'That's not like you, Harry. What's got into you?'

'Maybe the realisation of my own mortality, and the desire to live a little while I still can.' They were brave words, spoken confidently, but Falconer didn't put the conviction into them that he should have done.

'Good man. You go for it.' Doc Christmas,

unaware of just how tentatively the explanation had been vocalised, had donned his gown, hat, and mask, and was now scrubbing up for his 'cut and rummage' – another of his expressions. 'Good luck.'

Falconer endured the inevitable and, at long last, picked up his keys, donned his coat, which he had hung up behind the doctor's office door, and left the premises. He didn't really relish going back to the station and headed, instead, for Fallow Fold, where a lady vicar of his acquaintance lived. Maybe talking to the Reverend Florrie Feldman would make him feel easier in himself about Green's untimely departure. And where, exactly, was Carmichael this morning? He hadn't turned up like the angel of death at his usual time to haunt the office. Then he remembered that his sergeant had booked a day off to attend an antenatal appointment with Kerry, and would not be in until the next morning.

DC Tomlinson finished his enquiries about the 'lifting' of all the recently acquired 'Christmas presents' at the addresses he had been sent to, then went on a door-to-door enquiry, to see if any of the neighbours had noticed anything. All the burgled families had been away at the times of the thefts, and someone, who had obviously cased the joints in advance, had taken his chance. Tomlinson had little hope of any success, but at least it kept him away from the station and distracted him from more maudlin thoughts.

The newest member of the CID team, Neil Tomlinson, had arrived at the station following his request for a transfer to be nearer to his girlfriend, Imogen. The opportunity had come when his predecessor, the somewhat hapless DC Roberts, had requested a transfer back to Manchester. He was feeling much more settled now he had been in the area for a few months.

Being sent out to follow up the burglaries had been a relief. The thief, or thieves, had targeted homes with more than one car, and where the members of the household, together with one of the cars, were away for the holidays. They had always struck after dark, so there was less chance of them being spotted. If they were, they would probably be taken for a family member returned home and in need of late night transport. The fact that they took the remaining car stuffed with all their valuables just added insult to injury.

There had been half a dozen of these burglaries reported so far, each having been discovered when the occupants returned home from their New Year breaks, and four of the stolen cars had already been located, abandoned and burnt out, but there were two still unaccounted for.

In this, and other somewhat fruitless pastimes, the days after Merv Green's funeral passed, finally drawing to their uneventful and dismal conclusion.

The next morning, after a scalding hot cup of tea, Carmichael was out in the woods again with his dogs. The thaw was more pronounced now, and the ground was becoming muddy, making him wish he'd taken the time to put on his work boots. The dogs were, as always, running hither and thither, pursuing scent trails that eventually led nowhere, and he let them off the lead for a bit to get some exercise that did not involve his own body being dragged in full pursuit.

After he had stood for quite a few minutes in melancholy thought, he called them, but only Dipsy came back, his little legs working like fury to achieve a movement that was as close to a run as he could manage, but which produced little speed. Of the Great Dane there was neither sight nor sound. Raising his hands to cup his mouth, Carmichael shouted, 'Mulligan,' his call echoing through the bare trees. This was very similar to the outbreak of rebellion in which the two had indulged the day before. In the summer the foliage would have dulled and absorbed the volume, but in this season of the year, it carried loud and clear on the still air.

There was still no response, so he reattached Dipsy's lead and marched off in the direction in which the big dog had headed when his leash was removed, Dipsy's legs working like crazy to keep up. Carmichael whistled loudly to attract the animal's attention, and occasionally stopped to call his name again. Where had that dratted animal got to? He was usually easy to locate, having stopped to sniff at some wild animal droppings or a local dog's markings.

Carmichael finally found Mulligan digging furiously under a clump of withered bracken next to a goodly patch of brambles, not short of a thorn or two even in January. He put on the dog's lead and attempted to drag the animal away, but there was no way Mulligan was giving up what he had found, and he whined and

25

pulled, still clawing at the earth under the plant.

'What are you worrying at there, boy?' asked Carmichael. He let the lead go slack, and squatted down, so that he could see if there was anything under the dead undergrowth that had particularly attracted the dog's attention, or whether he was in one of his silly moods – such as when he apparently attempted to dig his way to Australia, something he did often in the back garden of Jasmine Cottage.

He had managed to scrape away quite a lot of earth, and gleaming in the dark soil was something of a much lighter shade. It looked a totally different texture as well. 'Come away, Mulligan,' Carmichael said in his do-as-you're-damned-well-told voice. Mulligan desisted, looking round at his new master with a quizzical frown on his canine face. The big man didn't normally speak to him in that tone, and he was puzzled as to what he had done wrong. His family knew he liked to dig in case there was something exciting underground that he had not known about.

Carmichael moved a few steps away and called the beast to heel, then unleashed the command, 'Sit!' Meekly, the Great Dane sat, his example being followed by Dipsy Daxie, although from the front end there was little change in the dachshund's appearance.

From a coat pocket, Carmichael pulled out the tool with which he had cleared his windscreen of ice daily before the thaw, and which he had forgotten to put back inside the car, and scraped gently round what the dog had uncovered. It was not buried deeply, and where he found resistance, he felt round it to see what was causing the problem. After only a few minutes he had un-covered something round and pale that looked suspiciously like the top of a skull. It wasn't one belonging to any woodland animal he knew of – it was far too big for that – but it was definitely not farm animal shaped either. There was something about it that was horribly familiar...

His immediate instinct was to cover what he had found and call for back-up, and he tore off some of the undergrowth which had died for the winter, and covered the discoloured dome with it. That done, he made for home as fast as he could to drop off the dogs. He also pulled out his mobile phone from his pocket to give the boss a ring on the way. If that skull wasn't human, he'd eat his desk, and although his appetite might be hearty enough, he would have some trouble digesting the wood and metal.

When Falconer's mobile rang, he was sitting with a latte and a Danish pastry in a coffee shop, unusually playing hooky. His mind teeming with possible explanations of where he was and what he was doing there, none of them honest, he was glad to hear Carmichael's voice. Why, he asked himself, did he feel so guilty? He should only just have arrived at the office. So he was skiving! He'd already been to his desk, taken a report, and sent Tomlinson off to investigate, and he deserved a bit of a break, having arrived at work at sparrow-fart. He just didn't fancy the canteen for once.

'Hello, Carmichael. Were you looking for me?'

'No, sir. I haven't left home yet. It's just that I've

found, or rather, the dogs have uncovered, something in the local patch of woodland, and I think it's a human skull. I don't want to disturb it anymore, but I thought someone else ought to see it. I'll be happy if I'm wrong, but I don't think I am.'

'Where are you now?' This was better than going into the station of mourning. 'Are you in the cottage? Have you left your discovery unattended?'

'I'm on my way back to drop off the dogs. I covered what was dug up with some undergrowth I detached, and I don't think there was anyone around when I left.'

'Good man. Get yourself back there to guard it, and I'll ring you when I reach the woodland, so that you can guide me in.'

'I'll leave in about fifteen minutes so I don't have too long to hang about in the miserable weather. Give me a ring when you get here,' requested Carmichael with eminent common sense.

'Will do. I'll be with you as soon as I can.'

Falconer ended the call and paid his bill, a cautious smile forming round his mouth. This could be just the distraction they needed. Consulting his watch, he rang Tomlinson on his mobile, and told him to pursue whatever he could, whether it was house-to-house enquiries, or paperwork. He and Carmichael would be in as soon as they could. At the other end of the phone the new DC was rather pleased about this, as he would not be subjected to their melancholy influence for a while longer.

Falconer roared out of Market Darley, giving the journey to Castle Farthing a thrashing in his Porsche Boxster, just because he could, and the sound of the engine and the speed improved his mood. For now, he would take out his grief and frustrated helplessness on the road. He looked forward to being alone with Carmichael at the beginning of what might prove to be a case of murder: not that he wished anybody ill, and if it was merely bones that his sergeant had unearthed, or rather that his dogs had dug up, they were unlikely to be recent.

When he got to Castle Farthing, he parked his car outside Carmichael's double-fronted cottage so as not to draw attention to himself, then strolled over towards the woods, whistling almost innocently. Entering the trees he went directly ahead, then rang Carmichael to let him know he was already in the woods. The trilling of the phone seemed to be not quite straight ahead, but over to the right.

When his call was answered, he instructed, 'End the call and let me ring you again, Sergeant, but don't answer it. Let me use the ring tone as an aural beacon.'

'A what?'

'Just do as you're told. If it stops ringing and starts again, answer it.'

'Yes, sir.' Carmichael was quite hurt at being so summarily dealt with.

His phone began to ring, and he held it out in front of him so that it could be heard more clearly. If he'd really been in a huff he would have buried it in his pocket, then seen how easy he was to find. Of the inspector, he heard no sound. After about a minute, the ringing stopped, and he could hear a rustling through the trees over to his left. 'Over here, sir,' he called, making quite a rustling sound himself, for guidance.

The phone rang again and he answered it. 'Did you hear me calling, sir?' he asked, eager once more to get on with things.

'No, I've heard nothing but a faint ring tone.'

'But there was rustling in the bushes and undergrowth that I thought was you, and I rustled back. Sir, why am I whispering?'

'No idea. Perhaps you could come to the northern edge of the woods and lead me in. That would probably be the easiest way to do this. Come and get me. I seem to be lost.' It took a lot for him to be able to admit that after all the years he had spent in the army, but he did not have a compass, and had not been concentrating as hard as he should have been on his direction. His thoughts really did need focus.

'Yes, sir.'

As Carmichael ended the call, the thing that had been making the rustling noise to which he provided an answer in kind, looked at him from a few yards away. As soon as he moved, the deer wandered off, soon getting lost in the entwined bare branches that provided such a grateful screening for him and his kind.

Carmichael grinned widely at this unexpected encounter with wildlife, and started off in search of the inspector, whom he found, looking like a lost soul, on a tree stump not far from the road.

A fine drizzle began to fall, and as Carmichael led the inspector off towards the remains they got steadily wetter and wetter. 'This is worse than real rain,' commented Falconer huffily. 'You seem to get more easily soaked than you do in the stuff with bigger drops.'

'Here we are, sir,' replied Carmichael who had not been listening. 'It's just under that pile of dead bracken.'

Carmichael pulled back the fronds, revealing what Mulligan had uncovered earlier, and pointed for Falconer's benefit, in case he should have become blind in the recent past.

'I can see for myself, Sergeant, and, yes, it does look like the top of a human skull,' the inspector snapped, kneeling to examine the object more closely. 'Damn it. We might need the services of a forensic anthropologist for this, to determine whether the remains are recent or ancient, maybe preserved by the soil. I'll arrange first for Doc Christmas to come out and see what he thinks, and I'll get a Uniform to guard the remains while we wait for him and a CSI team.'

'Looks like murder to me, sir.'

'It would be a very obliging suicide that had so conveniently buried itself in such a tidy way, wouldn't it, sergeant?'

'Sorry, sir. Didn't think.' A blue bubble began to emerge from the sergeant's mouth.

'Is that what I think it is, Carmichael?'

''Uff, fir,' replied the sergeant, his mouth otherwise engaged in trying to disentangle itself from the emerging bubble.

'Put it in a scrap of paper and dispose of it when you're near a bin. Do *not* throw it on the ground, and please don't chew it again when you're on duty.'

Carmichael spat into a tissue that he removed from his pocket, and blushed to have been found

31

out, although he hadn't really been on duty when he'd left home to take the dogs for a walk, and he'd had it in his mouth since then. 'Sorry, sir.'

'I should think so too. How many times have I asked you not to chew that revolting stuff in my presence?'

'Don't know, sir.'

'It must have been dozens, if not hundreds. Leave that sort of thing to the kids.'

'They don't like it.'

'And very sensible they are, too.'

'Yes, sir.'

'I will not have an officer on duty looking like a cow chewing the cud.'

'No, sir.' Carmichael looked suitably chastised.

Falconer made a couple of quick phone calls, and they settled in to wait for a relief officer. 'If they're ancient,' he mused, 'we'll be off the hook. In fact, if they're more than a few decades old, it won't be for us to solve. If, however, they've been buried within the last few years, it's up to us to identify the victim – if victim it be, although I don't suppose somebody just curled up and died here – and find the killer.

'I rather hope they're not too old. There's nothing harder than trying to identify the remains of someone who died more than twenty years ago. Even ten years is a bit of a struggle. However, if they prove to be our problem, we can start with the MisPer list. You might have put us on to something here.'

'Unless it's someone who was a bit of a loner and had never been reported missing,' retorted Carmichael, unable to remember how to look on the bright side at the moment.

'You are a cheerful little soul today, aren't you?' Falconer snapped, momentarily demotivated. 'If that turns out to be the case we'll have to work even harder, won't we, if we're to come up with a victim and the murderer. We could certainly do with something to get our teeth into at the moment, though; something to stop us thinking too hard about Green and the pointlessness of life.'

Ignoring this pessimistic view similar to his own, Carmichael replied disconnectedly, 'I should have brought back a trowel when I went home. At least with that we could have dug out a bit more.'

'I think we'd better leave that to the specialists, don't you?' Falconer had visions of what had happened a few years ago at a rather ancient cemetery near the river, where the records of grave depths had not been accurately recorded. One grave that had been indicated as a triple, originally dug nine feet deep, had turned out to be only a single when it was opened to inter another body. This made it only four-and-a-half feet before the last interment, and a rather over-enthusiastic gravedigger had removed his fork from the earth with one of its tines through an eye socket, the skull dangling from his fork like a bone charm.

This inevitability had been made obvious when the proximity to the river was noted, and the level of the water table, but it had been a disturbing incident. When Doc Christmas had told them about it, Falconer had thought it must have been a horrifying experience for the digger – but Carmichael had only commented that he didn't understand why they hadn't been using a mechanical digger to get out the bulk of the earth.

They only had to wait about twenty minutes before the lumbering figure of PC John Proudfoot came crashing through the dead undergrowth: nearing retirement, overweight, and out of condition, Proudfoot was the man whom Falconer had once described as not having two brain cells to rub together.

Out of breath, he puffed, 'They've put off the doc's arrival until after they've properly unearthed them there remains. You'll just have to wait for him.'

Immediately irritated by the constable's news, Falconer replied, 'Wait? We may have to, but *we* don't have to do it here in this beastly drizzle,' implying that Proudfoot would just have to put up and shut up. 'We'll be off to Carmichael's cottage and have a bit of a dry and a hot drink. Carry on, Constable.'

As he stalked off, Carmichael trailing behind in his wake, the sergeant commented quietly, 'That was a bit sharp, wasn't it, sir?'

'Just looking at him annoys me. How they think he can cover for Green, I have no idea. And we haven't got the excellent Starr anymore. What is the force coming to?'

'They can't just magic new personnel out of thin air, sir.'

'Well, they should be able to.'

There was no chance of a civilised conversation with the inspector when he was in this mood and Carmichael hoped that the presence of a roaring fire and a mug of tea would lift his spirits, as they were now thoroughly soaked.

Kerry Carmichael heaved her heavily pregnant body to the door to let them in and, summing up Falconer's mood in a couple of seconds, declared, 'I'll put the kettle on, shall I?'

Although the inspector expected to be assaulted by dogs, three small ones, what he did not expect was Mulligan the Great Dane to leap up and wash his face with huge enthusiasm, while Dipsy Daxie made short work of his shoelaces.

Taking the only option of salvation in the face of salivation open to him, he spun round and threw himself face down on the sofa, calling for a clean, wet flannel and a hand towel. He stipulated 'clean' because the idea of rubbing his face with one that had already been used by one of the inhabitants of the cottage made his skin crawl. He could be fastidious at times, and the present situation was absolutely disgusting. He had a complete dread of dog saliva, and now had it in his hair, on his face, and in his mouth and nostrils. It didn't help things when Carmichael called out, 'No tongues, there's a good boy, Mulligan.'

'Down, Mulligan!' Kerry shouted. 'Kitchen. In your bed,' she ordered as she brought the necessary equipment for Falconer to clean himself up, then dragged Dipsy Daxie after the huge hound and into the food preparation area.

'What the dickens is that hellhound doing here?' the inspector mumbled through the flannel as he scrubbed at his face. 'Is he on holiday with you – again?'

'Actually, he lives with us now, sir,' replied Carmichael in as apologetic a tone as he could manage. He absolutely adored the Great Dane, and couldn't understand why his superior was so negative about the animal, but had not mentioned to him yet the details of the canine swap.

'It's like this, sir; his owners are getting on a bit, and Mulligan hasn't stopped growing yet and needs an awful lot of exercise. I consulted with Kerry and the boys and then suggested that if we swapped Mistress Fang and Mr Knuckles for Mulligan, we could take on the bigger dog. The neighbours would get the canine company they need, with less exercise to provide, and the boys could go and take out the little dogs whenever they felt like it, with Mulligan's old mummy and daddy able to visit him if and when they wanted.'

'Carmichael, you're a soft-headed chump. And I suppose I have to run the gamut of this licky giant every time I visit, now?' Although Falconer was horrified by this information, he was glad the little dogs had been passed on. He had always considered that a man of Carmichael's bulk with such tiny creatures as those were on leads resembled a man with a couple of wasps on strings: visually ridiculous, as well as being impractical and downright dangerous from the dogs' point of view.

'Yes, sir. Sorry, sir,' Carmichael said, although he wasn't in the least repentant. He was delighted with how things had turned out. He had been getting a little irritated about how often he had tripped over the Yorkshire Terrier and the Chihuahua, and he'd always lusted after owning a magnificent animal like Mulligan. It was just unfortunate that the inspector didn't share his enthusiasm for such a stupendous specimen. 'And he's not fully grown yet,' he added, as if this were a bonus.

'If he grows any bigger you'll be able to enter him for the St Leger,' said Falconer.

Kerry saved the situation by calling, 'Tea up!' from the kitchen. The two men went to stand by the fire, gently steaming, as its heat dried out their trouser legs. The inspector decided that he was in a state that he could tolerate until lunchtime, when he could go home for a shower and a change of clothes.

A little later, but still in the cottage, Falconer received a call from what they were already thinking of as the crime scene, saying that a few pieces of jewellery had been found with the remains, and this gave an indication that the death had not been associated with robbery.

'Apparently there's an ankle chain, a cross on a neck chain, and a signet ring, all in gold,' he informed Carmichael. 'I suggest we go and collect the evidence bag and contact Wanda Warwick to see if she can identify them: they could turn out to be from that young woman from Shepford St Bernard that she reported missing to us. I'll call in at home on the way for a shower, before I come back to the office to pick you up.' He could still feel the ghost of the saliva with which he had been dripping, and wouldn't relax until he'd thoroughly expunged it from his person.

'Shall I call her, sir?'

'No. You just get a file opened on the case and make sure Doc Christmas is alerted. I'll go and collect the evidence; you head back to the office.'

When Falconer returned to the scene, there was a team carefully excavating the remains, using small trowels and brushes to clear away the dirt encrusting them, and the jewellery was encased in a plastic evidence bag ready for identification.

By the time Falconer felt clean again and returned to the station, Carmichael informed him that Doc Christmas had paid a visit to the site. Christmas had declared the remains to be fairly recent, and that they were now being carefully lifted so that the doctor could make a closer inspection of them and the incident reported to the Coroner. With that information, Falconer could now telephone Wanda Warwick with a view to calling round to her house, Ace of Cups, in Shepford St Bernard, to see if she could confirm whether the jewellery that had been found with the remains had belonged to the missing Bonnie Fletcher.

Chapter Three

It was with a heavy heart that he knocked on the door of Ace of Cups. He was dreading showing the gold items to its occupant. Bonnie Fletcher had been Wanda Warwick's best friend, and she would take it hard to see the items of jewellery in such tragic circumstances, for he had convinced himself that their victim was the young woman who had disappeared from her cottage in the village almost a year ago exactly.

Wanda looked, initially, pleased to see him, and it was only when he was settled in an armchair with a cup of coffee that a cloud of anxiety appeared on her face.

'Is it something about Bonnie?' she asked. 'Have you found her?'

Without a word of explanation, Falconer reached into his pocket and removed the plastic evidence bag. 'Do you recognise any of these pieces of jewellery?' he asked, handing it to the concerned woman.

Wanda examined the gold objects, her worried expression turning to one of puzzlement. 'Not at all,' she replied. 'Why? Did you think they were Bonnie's?'

His mind partly taken up with the words 'damn', 'bum', and other such mild expletives, Falconer gently explained that he thought they had found her friend's remains, but was very happy to tell her that he hadn't. And now, he thought, he had a body to identify. He'd have to pursue the identity of the remains through dental records and check up on missing persons within the last few years. They certainly hadn't been buried there yesterday.

With his face indicating relief and his mind swirling with possibilities about exactly whose remains Carmichael's gigantic dog had unearthed, he decided to chase up his sergeant about getting on to Missing Persons, and get Tomlinson on to the local dentists from Market Darley to Carsfold. With any luck he wouldn't have to go further afield, but he had a small corner of his mind toying with the idea that her teeth might have to go nationwide – he presumed it was a 'she', with the type of jewellery that the remains had been wearing.

After refusing, as politely as possible, another cup of coffee, he returned to his office to find that Doc Christmas had confirmed the remains to be female, belonging to a woman in her late twenties to early thirties who had never given birth. X-rays had been taken of her teeth and were already being circulated to local dentists, this latter task being the work of Tomlinson, who was proving to be on the ball when it came to working off his own bat.

Carmichael had also had a surge of independent thought, and was already looking at reports of missing persons over the last few years, Doc Christmas having said that the remains were only a few years old. The body was not particularly decomposed, although the top of the head had been nibbled at by wildlife, and one of the hands was missing, probably unearthed and chewed off by a fox or something similar. If there was no result, he would look back further, before the hunt was extended to other police areas.

Falconer, feeling slightly redundant, nipped out to have his hair trimmed before his dinner date with Honey. He was determined to look his best and had decided that his hair, being long enough to comb now, was rather on the long side and could do with a tidy-up. The army had left him with a horror of having long, luxuriant locks.

He also called into the Market Darley branch of a gentlemen's outfitters and purchased a new shirt and tie, determined that he should not fall short sartorially. That he was considering wearing such garments at all on a date was an indication of his innate formality of occasion: he would no sooner go for dinner in a polo shirt than he would put on a tutu and attempt to dance *Swan Lake*.

When he returned to his desk, it was to find that Carmichael had discovered no females in the projected age group from those who had been reported missing in their area during the time period, who had not either returned home or contacted friends or relatives, so that proved to be a dead end. Information from the dental practitioners would have to wait a bit longer, and he fiddled about with file notes until the end of the day.

Before he left the office, he made one request of his sergeant. 'When I visit your home in future, will you make sure that that four-footed canine fiend is locked out of the main room? It's not as if you've got a hallway that I can shelter in while he's restrained.'

'Will do, sir,' replied Carmichael with a smile and not a trace of guilt at the assault upon his superior officer earlier that day. He loved Mulligan unconditionally, and could not understand why everyone else didn't do so too.

Falconer dressed with special care that evening, determined to ascertain exactly how he felt about the way things were going, but had no idea how he would decide: he just knew he needed to look his best so that he could take a proper look at things. Dressing well made him feel at ease and able to judge matters more clearly. Disarray in his appearance was a distraction he didn't need.

Dr Honey Dubois lived in an apartment in a modern block not far from the town centre, on the first floor and, much to his approval, every part of her home was immaculate. Her furniture was modern and stylish, her carpets and blinds spotless; not a thing was out of place. There were no magazines or newspapers left around, and even her handbag was neatly placed by the side of the sofa so as not to cause obstruction or be an eyesore.

The conversation flowed relatively easily. Her cooking was Caribbean in style, but not too hot, and he was fed well. The woman, too, was as blemish-free as her home, and her hair was in recently woven corn-rows, her make-up immaculate. She smelt of freesias. What was not to like? She was very attractive and would probably make a remarkable wife and mother. But, still, he had doubts about how he really felt.

That evening he enjoyed a particularly well-cooked meal and good company, but when she asked him if he would stay the night, he was overcome with shyness, and only said he would think about it for the future. He was surprised that he had not spent the whole evening in a state of nervous tension, wondering if she would invite him to share her bed, and when it happened, he was almost relieved as he turned her down as politely as possible.

That was just something he didn't do, and wouldn't, until he was sure that he had found the right person. And, at the moment, he wasn't certain. Heather, his previous sort-of-girlfriend and a nurse, had not been 'the one' either. Never mind about today's lax attitude of not even knowing the name of the person with whom one was communing sexually: he had been brought up in a much more old-fashioned way and thought anything else would be un-gentlemanly and completely amoral.

She accepted his decision gracefully, knowing well what he had been like when their relationship first started, then stalled, then started again. She didn't want to rush him into anything with which he wasn't comfortable but, in her opinion, he was too moral for his own good and for hers, too.

He left her home still slightly uneasy, with a feeling that he had a lot of deep thinking to do about his attitude to women in general and Honey in particular. He resolved to try to be more relaxed in future, and attempt to see things from her point of view, being less intransigent in his outlook, but when he reached home he was in a foul mood about his stubborn attitude to relationships. Hence, he sat for over an hour on the sofa stroking his cats and playing with them before relaxing enough to go to bed. This was mainly due to his Abyssinian, Monkey, who persistently reached her face up to his and rubbed her cheeks against his jaw, while making a strange little chirruping noise.

Finally, at peace and relaxed in the knowledge that at least one creature loved him unconditionally, he retired to bed.

Early the next morning there was news from a dental practice in Market Darley that they had matched the teeth to a client named Annie Symons, a thirty-three-year-old woman who had

43

lived at number two Drovers Lane in Castle Farthing. She had not been in for a check-up since December 2008, and the dentist had put her records into a group that was to be given warning of being struck off his list. Having been given the time-frame involved, however, he had decided to have a look, as she could not reasonably have been expected to see him if she had disappeared a few years ago.

Tomlinson was immediately dispatched to talk to the dentist to see if he could remember anything about her; and Falconer and his sergeant set off for Castle Farthing to question the residents of Drovers Lane about their former neighbour.

Drovers Lane was the first turning on the right off the western branch of the High Street as they came in from the direction of Market Darley. Number one was the general store, 'Allsorts', number two being situated on the same side, just across an alleyway and opposite the garden of the public house, The Fisherman's Flies.

Castle Farthing had been the situation for Falconer's first case with Carmichael as his sergeant, nearly three years earlier, and he thought back to the events of that summer. Allsorts was still run by Rosemary Wilson, but the garage opposite which had been run by Michael Lowry was still closed for business and awaiting either a new proprietor – unlikely – or redevelopment, currently blocked by the planning committee. It had been re-opened briefly just over a year ago, but had been closed again after only a few months by the chain that had acquired it due to the economic downturn and unprofitability. The garage remained unmentioned by Falconer, out of tact, as Lowry had been Kerry Carmichael's first husband and father of her two boys.

The inspector decided that they would tackle the shopkeeper first, as she was at the heart of the spider's web of local gossip and events. Leaving Carmichael to speak to his wife on his own later, to avoid further contact with the infamous Mulligan, they entered the premises and found the owner looking full of beans behind the counter. What a shop! There was just about everything that a customer could want in there: from aniseed balls to brooms and gardening tools. It was an Aladdin's cave that its owner could be rightly proud of, and she beamed at the two of them as they entered her shop.

The business had been failing when Falconer had first met Rosemary Wilson, but she had installed a Lotto machine, persuaded a national bank to install a cash dispenser in the exterior wall of the premises, and started selling scratchcards and alcohol. The licence had been granted without fuss as the only other source of this vital commodity was from The Fisherman's Flies. That wasn't open all hours, as the little shop was, and now many more people were tempted inside to make urgent purchases instead of going to the cash machines in Market Darley and using the supermarket. Of course, they still didn't do a large shop, but business had picked up sufficiently for her to feel comfortable about profits, now she was actually making some.

'Hello there, young Davey. And what can I do for you today? Kerry keeping well? I haven't seen the lads in for a while for their sweeties. I hope they haven't been naughty.'

'Hello, Rosemary,' Carmichael greeted her.

'Good morning, Mrs Wilson. We're just making enquiries about a young woman who used to live next door at number two. Her name was Annie Symons, and we believe that she may have moved away.' Falconer was keeping the mood light as he didn't want to give away too much information.

'Was that who you found yesterday in the woods?' asked the woman, her finger firmly on the village pulse.

'Did you know her at all?' countered Falconer, ignoring the question.

'Haven't seen her for about ... let me see ... about three years or more,' replied Mrs Wilson. 'Has she been murdered then?'

'Did she come in here often?' enquired Falconer, not at all seduced by the leading questions.

'She used to pop in for bits and pieces – usually on her way to work. She did fill-in bar work at The Fisherman's Flies for George and Paula.' The named pair were the couple who ran the local pub and were very popular in the village; ex-Londoners, they had both been taken to Castle Farthing's heart and were accepted as honorary locals.

'Did she have a full-time job, or did she just do odd hours?'

'She did hours at other local pubs if staff had let them down, but I don't remember her having any other regular work. I don't really know what she did with her time.'

'Could you describe her to us?' Falconer wanted a picture of what the victim looked like, and

46

Carmichael hadn't been married to Kerry when this woman seemed to have disappeared. He was still at home with his parents. He lived in a ramshackle extension at the back of the property that Falconer always thought of as 'Carmichael Towers'; there not really being room for him in the main council house, not only due to the number of family members, but also because of his size.

'She was a slight girl. She had, as I remember, short black hair and green eyes, just like a cat's. I believe she had been married once, but was divorced, and she wasn't a young girl, neither was she middle-aged. I'd suppose her to be in her early thirties.'

'Is there someone in the property now?'

'An elderly couple have been there for a few years now. Nice, regular customers, they are; always forgetting something when they go to the supermarket.'

'Do you know of any relatives or friends?' They'd have to find somebody to contact, wouldn't they? But it seemed that this young woman had lived an isolated life, hardly ever going out, except to work and, although she had been married, had divorced and lost touch with her ex-husband.

'If it's any help to you, the owner of the cottage asked me to take in a few boxes of her things so that he could re-let it. I've got the stuff in my stockroom out back.' This last was offered as if it would be of no interest to the two detectives, but Falconer seized it as a dog does a bone.

'That's marvellous, Mrs Wilson. Could you show us where they are?'

As she led the way, she asked after Kerry and

47

casually patted Carmichael on the back at the thought of the birth of the twins. 'You know I'm always available for baby-sitting, don't you, Davey boy?'

The cardboard boxes were a little tattered by the passage of time, but they yielded a few photographs, a couple of which seemed to be recent, and could be used in an effort to find anyone who knew her. There was also, incongruously, a copy of the *Carsfold Gazette*, and Falconer couldn't understand why it had been kept, unless it had just been shoved in there to get rid of it. It did help with when she had last been around, though, as it was dated early May 2009. Their next stop would be The Fisherman's Flies, followed by visits to the other residents of Drovers Lane.

George Covington was just pulling the heavy door bolts to open the pub for midday when they arrived, and he ushered them in, calling to his wife Paula that there were visitors from the police. She rushed out from the back room, patting her hair and rubbing together her lips to indicate that she had just given them another coat of coral-coloured lipstick.

It was darker inside than it was outside due to the nature of the small windows and their tiny panes, but light from the real log fire twinkled on horse-brasses and copper warming pans, and made the old wood of the bar, polished within an inch of its life, glow in rich tones. Large baskets of logs were either side of the hearth, ready to be thrown on to replenish the blaze. This feature proved a magnet for customers, most of whom no longer had open fires in their homes, and were fascinated by the flames.

The two detectives ignored this distraction and, instead, seated themselves on stools at the bar. The blaze might interfere with their concentration, so mesmerising was it, and they had the beguiling hit of dancing flames at Jasmine Cottage and in the house in Letsby Avenue to look forward to.

"Ello, gents. And what brings you here this drizzly, grey day? Trouble, is there? I'd 'eard that there 'ad been a body found in the woods, but the news 'asn't got round yet about who it was. What's the goss?' Paula always got straight to the point, and didn't fiddle-faddle around with social niceties.

'Going for the jugular, as usual,' commented Falconer.

'I can't be doin' with all that goin' round the 'ouses with all that nonsense about askin' if folks 'ave 'ad a nice day, and 'ow are the budgies getting' on. I want to know what's 'appenin' without no frilly bits.'

'Paula, don't be so rude,' interjected her husband.

'I'm not bein' rude. I'm just askin' the man to call a spade a spade,' she replied, with a flounce of her newly permed hair.

'We believe that you used to employ Annie Symons from Drovers Lane behind the bar as a relief worker.'

'That's right. Oh, it weren't 'er who were found in the woods, was it?' asked George, an expression of concern on his face.

'It was indeed, and she seemed to have been there for some time. We've spoken to Mrs Wilson

49

at the shop, and we wondered what you could tell us about Annie.' Falconer could also get straight on to the matter at hand.

'She were a good worker. Always glad to 'ave her fillin' in, we was, and if she 'adn't disappeared so suddenly, we'd 'ave offered her a full-time position. She got on very well with the punters, did Annie.'

Falconer had a sudden vision of the dead woman surrounded by young men in straw boaters with long, wooden poles in their hands, which he had to shake his head to dismiss. 'When did you last see her?'

'Oh, that's a question, that is. I'll 'ave to take a look in me books to find that out, but I'll do that later when you've told us what's goin' on. Paula, love, go an' 'ave a glance in the records and see when Annie last did a shift for us.'

'You do it yourself, George Covington. I'm not goin' out the back and missin' all the fun,' she replied with a rebellious look.

'We don't really know anything yet.' Falconer decided to be very upfront, because he knew that this bar was a wonderful source of information, if he'd let it be. 'She'd obviously been there for some time, so we'd like to pinpoint the last time she was seen alive.'

'Paula, you go and make the gentlemen a cup of coffee, and I'll chase up that date, then we can get down to business.'

Soon, steaming cups in front of them and the date 17th May 2009 in Carmichael's notebook, George unexpectedly volunteered a useful titbit of information. 'She used to do fill-in work in

50

Stoney Cross at The Inn on the Green – d'you know Tarquin and Peregrine?'

Falconer remembered them well from an early case he and his sergeant had worked on; which coincided with the first time in his life that he had fallen in love. Today was really bringing up people from the past. Serena Lyddiard's face suddenly flooded his consciousness, and he felt he could even smell her perfume. Reluctantly he pushed the image away from his mind and concentrated instead on the pair of landlords.

Tarquin Radcliffe and Peregrine McKnight, who ran The Inn on the Green together, were built like rugby players but were, incongruously, rather camp. The landlord broke the short silence that had occurred by informing them, 'I thought she'd gone orf to look after a sick relative, and Paula thought she'd packed orf to live in Australia with a cousin of hers but, looking back, she were an awkward girl who never seemed to visit anyone, and I can't see her doin' either of those things. What do you reckon, Paula?'

'I don't know about a sick relative, but I know she 'ad a cousin in Australia. That's why I thought she must've gone there.'

Oh no, thought Falconer, not Australia. They'd be at it for ever if they had to trace a mysterious relative on the other side of the world – one who probably didn't even share the same surname, especially as the victim had been married and they'd no evidence that she'd reverted back to her maiden name.

'Did you know anything about her life and what she did in her spare time?' asked Falconer.

'No,' they said together, George picking up the promised narrative. 'That's what I meant about 'er being good with the punters. She never talked about 'erself, but drew out the customers, and got them to talk about themselves. You wouldn't believe 'ow popular that made her. People so like talkin' about themselves that they can entertain themselves all day doing just that, and Annie understood that.'

She would have made a good detective, thought Falconer, trying to think of anything else he could ask. 'Do you know of anywhere else she might have worked apart from the pub in Stoney Cross?'

'Can't say that I do,' replied the publican, 'although maybe Peregrine and Tarquin can be more forthcoming.'

'We'll nip over there after we've had a word with her old neighbours.' With that, the two policemen made their exit.

As it was now lunchtime, Carmichael phoned ahead to Kerry to ask her to shut Mulligan in the kitchen as they were coming over to eat their lunch – which Falconer would have to purchase first in the general store. He selected an unhealthy pork pie and a pre-packed salad from the refrigerated display and sighed as he crossed over to Jasmine Cottage. He'd been looking forward to lunch at home, as he had the remains of a salmon in the fridge which needed eating up, and that would have done him nicely as well as more healthily than the raised crust of the pie.

As Kerry admitted them a baying of distress and deprivation sounded through the door to the kitchen, but she slipped through and let Mulligan out into the garden: a distraction that proved an adequate compensation for missing his most-beloved person in the body of the inspector.

When she brought in tea, he asked her about Annie Symons. Had Kerry known her at all? Had they spent any time together? Had she planned to move away, or had she just disappeared? They could hardly not ask her anything, now that they were in the cottage, after all.

'I didn't know her very well,' Kerry replied, easing her bulk into a chair with a sigh of relief at getting off her feet, and continued, 'but we did have coffee together a couple of times before she went away – or rather, was murdered. How ghastly!'

Falconer was momentarily distracted by an urgent clawing at his right trouser leg as Dipsy Daxie, who had not been ejected from the living space, tried to scale his calf to achieve a comfortable place on his lap. As the inspector looked horrified, the sergeant scooped him up and sat him on his own lap, just missing setting him down on his plate of sandwiches. Falconer considered that Carmichael was the only person he knew with upper legs long enough to accommodate a dachshund lying along their length, its head resting happily on his stomach.

As he steadied his plate and checked its contents for paw prints, Kerry again spoke. 'She seemed a quiet woman who had had an unhappy marriage. I did get her to open up a couple of times when I encouraged her over here for a cuppa – that was before I met my Davey, and I don't think you two worked together then. It was before that dreadful old man next door got murdered; before we got the adjoining cottage and knocked through.

'She didn't have any children, and seemed to be quite happy with her own company, although I knew she occasionally went out on a date, just to dip her toe back into the water, so to speak – usually people she met when she was doing bar work and had had a chance to size them up.'

'Can you remember any of them?' asked Falconer, having to swallow a mouthful of his pork pie rather more quickly than was advisable, and coughing as a consequence. 'Do excuse me. Went down the wrong way.'

'Not offhand, but I could have a bit of a think about it. Do you think she could have been murdered by a man-friend then?'

'Much too early to say, but we have to take every possibility into account.'

'Of course. I don't think she really had many friends, and not much family to speak of, except for a cousin in Australia.' Falconer sighed inwardly. Was this blasted cousin the only person who was going to get a mention in the history of this woman's life and sorry death?

At this point, Carmichael scooped Dipsy Daxie on to the floor and suddenly sat down on the floor at Kerry's feet, leaning forward to put the side of his head on her enormous stomach, causing the dog to scramble to waddle over to him, whining plaintively. Falconer had no idea what was going on, and felt a flush of embarrassment creep up his face. Clearing his throat, he bent to stroke the dachshund to cover his flustered state, and Kerry spoke to reassure him that her husband had not suddenly gone mad.

'He's taking the opportunity to feel the babies move. He says that this is the only time they're going to get the opportunity to kick him in the head with his blessing.'

Falconer felt a renewal of his discomfiture, wondering how Carmichael could be so relaxed about his wife's state. Pregnancy was something about which he had always felt very uncomfortable, and would never have felt at ease enough to do this, even with a wife, had he had one. He envied the sergeant his easy-going outlook on life.

Ignoring Carmichael as he struggled to his feet, giving Kerry's bulge a final fondle with his right hand, Falconer said that, as he'd eaten his lunch, they ought to be off as they had to speak to the residents of Drover Lane, then go on to Stoney Cross to see the landlords of The Inn on the Green. Carmichael stuffed a whole sandwich into his mouth, having to insert the last of it with his thumbs, looking suddenly like a giant toad with an over-sized dragonfly, then tried to say something. Crumbs flew everywhere, much to Dipsy's delight, and the dog chased them the way he would snow.

'Wait until you've swallowed, man,' advised Falconer with exasperation. He may not have had a lot of experience of young children, but he was learning a lot from being nanny to Carmichael.

'I was going to ask Kerry to think about Annie Symons and we'd have a talk tonight, to see if she remembers anything about her in the meantime.'

'You just get back to work, Davey. I'll have to let Mulligan in soon, or he'll have tunnelled his way under the road to the pond, and be covered in weed and other filth when we get him out.' The thought of having to bathe Mulligan was a serious threat to his owner, as it was such a struggle, and Carmichael moved swiftly towards the front door so that Kerry could open the back one.

As they exited the warmth of the cottage, Falconer was struck again with Castle Farthing's prettiness, even in this dreary, cold winter weather. Its mix of roof tiles, slates, and thatch seemed to fit together as well as the pieces of a jigsaw puzzle, and the difference in finishes to the walls, be they stone, whitewash or brick, made a very pleasing sight. The place didn't look as if it had been cobbled together over a couple of centuries, but seemed as if this was meant – it was how it should be, and always had been.

Number two Drovers Lane was now occupied by a retired couple, the Walkers, who had moved from the south coast, having had enough of the seaside brigade in the warmer months, and wanting something different for their retirement.

'It was all crowds of trippers in the summer making the beaches too crowded to visit, with sea mists and breezes; and gloomy weather and drizzle in the winter, when nobody would want to walk there,' explained Mrs Walker, unnecessarily, in Falconer's opinion. He didn't need to know why they'd moved to Castle Farthing, just whether or not they had ever met Annie Symons.

'We moved inland because it's warmer in the summer and has more snow in winter. The coast is just too temperate and boring,' she added, even more superfluously.

'Mrs Walker, did you ever meet the previous

tenant of this property?' Falconer interrupted in desperation.

'She'd already done a moonlight flit when we first looked around the place,' she began. 'Seemed an odd thing to do at the time, seeing as how the landlord had just had the whole place redecorated. I wouldn't have left straight after that sort of facelift for the house, but there's no accounting for taste, is there? Perhaps she didn't like the colour. Furnished, it was then, but we had our own stuff, so we asked if it could be stored, so that we could have our own stuff about us. Taken us our whole lives to get nice pieces together to make a comfortable home, and we didn't want to have to give them up just because we'd moved.

'She'd been gone some time. The landlord said she just left without a word of warning. She didn't even stop paying her rent, but just took off and told nobody where she was going. He didn't know she was gone until he came over to do a routine inspection of the place, found it empty, and asked around a bit, to find out that no one had seen her for ages.'

They really must speak to the owner of the property, Falconer thought. And the continuation of the payment of rent would explain a lot. Annie Symons hadn't meant to leave her home so, therefore, had had no reason to cancel her regular payments to the owner.

Thanking Mrs Walker profusely for her information – more than he needed, nor, in fact, wanted – he dragged Carmichael away from his fascinated concentration on the life detail with which Mrs Walker was providing them, and up the short garden path of number three. Before he could knock at the door, the inspector's phone rang and he answered it to find Doc Christmas on the other end. 'Do you want to come in and have a look at these remains?' he asked in a jovial, conversational manner. 'They're fascinating. The eyes have gone, of course, but the pattern of decomposition is fascinating.'

'No way, Jose,' replied Falconer, ending the call rather abruptly and rapped firmly on the door-knocker. There was no answer. He knocked again and sent Carmichael round to the back to see if there was anyone in the kitchen. Mrs Walker popped out again and informed them that a builder lived there on his own, and would be out at work until after the light went, and later, if he was working indoors.

Number four proved to be owned by another retired couple, the Petersons, who had only lived there five months, and number five was empty. This wasn't getting them much further along. Numbers six, seven and eight also had no one at home, and Falconer was determined to get Tomlinson to come back here either out of working hours or at the weekend.

Leaving Castle Farthing in a cloud of exhaust fumes – he really needed either to change his car or have it serviced – the two detectives set off for Stoney Cross, only about two-and-a-half miles to the west, to speak to the landlords of The Inn on the Green.

Chapter Four

The public house with its attached restaurant was not quite as they remembered, having been given a fresh coat of white paint, its window frames and doors gleaming with a coat of new black gloss. It was a great oblong magpie of a building, but inviting. The inside had been similarly tarted-up, its scarred wooden floor having been replaced by trendy flagstones, the horse-brasses taken down, and armchairs had appeared in a variety of tartan upholstery.

Its huge fireplace, which used to hold only dried flowers and a screen, now boasted an over-sized gas log fire. No real logs for these two landlords. They may be of sufficient build for lugging them, but they wouldn't fancy getting splinters in their well-manicured hands. Without the sheer magic of burning logs this feature did, however, have its fair share of patrons who liked to sit and gaze at the gas-fed phenomenon. The place now looked thoroughly eclectic and modern, and boasted quite a few of the lunchtime clientele, either sitting with bar meals or at tables in the restaurant, bringing home to Falconer just how early they had eaten.

Tarquin Radcliffe and Peregrine McKnight were both present behind the bar genially dealing with orders, both big-framed and broad, wearing unexpected pastel colours. Both seemed to have put on a bit of timber since their last meeting, a combination of fat and muscle which was at odds with their camp behaviour.

'Hello, gentlemen,' Tarquin hailed them. 'Look, Perry, it's our favourite lawmen. What can we get you for your imbibing pleasure?'

'Two coffees. If you would be so good – oh, and the sugar bowl for DS Carmichael. We need to ask you a couple of questions.'

'How can we help you, dear hearts?' Peregrine had become even more 'mumsy' than before.

'We're making enquiries about the murder of a Ms Annie Symons, whom we believe used to work occasional shifts for you. We've already spoken to George and Paula Covington at The Fisherman's Flies in Castle Farthing, so we'd like to know when she last did a shift for you.'

'What, Annie, murdered? Do you hear that, Perry? How absolutely ghastly, Inspector,' said Tarquin.

'Frightful. Murder again, and only a couple of years after the last time. Whatever is life coming to in the countryside? This is hardly East End gang territory, now, is it?' commented Peregrine.

Both Falconer and Carmichael remained silent as the joint owners expressed their horror and surprise, fussing with some paper napkins in their disapproval.

'You check the records, and I'll get the coffees,' trilled Tarquin, waving them to a table and coming out from behind the bar. There may have been some doubt about this couple's relationship in the past, but there was none now. Tarquin had a thatch of sandy hair and brown eyes, and Peregrine, salt-and-pepper hair and greenish-hazel eyes, but apart from this they were now practically indistinguishable.

After consulting an iPad to access all their business records, Peregrine called across, 'April 12th 2009, for your information.'

'And you say she's been murdered?' asked Tarquin, still not quite taking in the information, as he returned with a tray with two steaming cups on it. Peregrine flapped a tea towel at a local to come and take over behind the bar while he left it for a good gossip.

As he joined them at the table, Carmichael was counting the spoonfuls of sugar that he dropped into his coffee, 'One, two three...' his tongue protruding from his mouth and muffling the numbers. Falconer confirmed the demise of their former staff member, drawing the unexpected piece of information from Tarquin that they had not had a lot of luck with their fill-in staff. 'We tried to get in touch with her for a bit of help when we had that big arts festival in Stoney Cross the other year, with all *that* murder and mayhem. You remember, that was when we first came across you two delightful chaps. But we had no luck, but we also couldn't get another of our occasional workers. It seems to have been a bad time for getting a bit of support behind the bar.'

'...four, five – six,' concluded the sergeant, as he started to stir the now turgid beverage.

Falconer took a few moments of silence, then asked them who this other member of staff was. It wasn't that he had a suspicious mind, but he had a nasty churning in his insides that he took to be a hunch, and he just had a feeling that

61

something was going to come of this remark. It could, however, just have been the mention of the Arts Festival, and he had to fight to get the image of Serena out of his mind and replace it with Honey's. Whatever was wrong with him? It was like this village was infested with memories.

'Suzie Doidge,' supplied Peregrine, determined not to be left out. 'She lives at King George III Terrace, or at least she did. She's not been near nor by since.'

'Could you tell me a bit about her?' Falconer's investigative instincts were up and running. What if it was not only two women who had disappeared? Far-fetched as this might sound, he didn't want to let this matter ride.

'All we know is what Reverend Ravenscastle told us.' Tarquin was back in the limelight.

'Pardon?'

'When we couldn't get hold of her – it seemed that her phone had been cut off. I say, that does sound like the old days, doesn't it – we asked the vicar, as he happened to be visiting this establishment, and he said he thought she'd left the area, although he didn't know where she'd gone or when, because she wasn't a church regular.'

'I shouldn't say this, but I believe she was claiming benefits and not declaring her shifts here. But I don't suppose it can do her any harm now she's gone away.' Peregrine really had his claws out now.

'And could you confirm the last shift *she* did for you?' asked the inspector, definitely on the hunt for a mystery.

Peregrine slipped back behind the bar, poked around on the iPad, and called out, 'Nothing since

Easter 2009, Inspector. April 10th, to be precise. It's so much easier to check these things since we transferred our paper records to the iPad. What a coincidence – both of them here on the same weekend. I never really thought about it before.'

Without turning a hair at this further endearment, Falconer replied, 'Many thanks for that, now could you tell us where can we find the vicar?' Carmichael was too busy to speak; concentrating instead on scooping out the last of the foam from his coffee from the side of the cup.

Tarquin suggested they try the vicarage and the church, and if they couldn't find him there to come back to see if he'd called in for afternoon tea. 'Very popular, we are, for afternoon tea, dear heart.'

'And could you remind us where these two properties are?' Falconer had to suppress a wince.

'Out of here, turn left; down School Lane to the T-junction with the High Street, then right and down a bit for the church, and the vicarage is just after it. You can't miss it.'

As they approached the vicarage, Falconer had a wave of memory. He was not surprised when a tall, gaunt man with thick, white, wavy hair, grey eyes, and glasses opened the door to them. From a distant room came a squawk of, ''Uck off.' Rev. Ravenscastle was the man with the cursing parrot.

'Just ignore Captain Bligh,' this apparition in the clerical collar advised them, and asked what he could do to help them. 'Don't I know you two?'

'Ge' stuffe',' floated down towards them.

'DI Falconer and DS Carmichael, sir,' replied the inspector, feeling the hairs on his head almost

stand on end as the bird shouted the unmention-
able 'see-you-next-Tuesday' word.

'I do apologise. Used to belong to a seagoing
gentleman of rather immoderate language, I'm
afraid. We can't be in control of all the things that
are willed to us, can we? And I couldn't bear to
have him destroyed just because his language is a
bit ripe. It's not as if he knows what he's saying,
is it?'

Falconer couldn't argue with this, presuming
that the vicar was referring to the parrot and not
its previous owner, and they followed him down
the hall and into his study, where he asked them to
take a seat and enquired how he could help them.

Not even knowing if the woman had disappeared or just been unavailable, Falconer felt
quite silly, but nevertheless asked the vicar about
Suzie Doidge.

'She's left the area,' Rev. Ravenscastle replied
curtly.

'Do you know when or where she went?'

'Quite a while ago, and I've no idea where.'

'Did you know her well?'

'Not at all.'

'How did you know she'd gone?'

'My wife, Adella, picked up the information at
the Mothers' Union.'

'How is your wife, sir?'

'Gone.'

'She's away?'

'No.'

'She's left you?' This last was asked very tentatively, as he considered it would be a sensitive
subject for a man of the cloth.

64

'She has departed this life,' came the curt reply.

'I'm so sorry, sir. Was it sudden, or was she ill?'

'She took her own life.'

There followed a stunned silence.

'She really perked up after that awful business a few years ago – you remember? That's when *we* met – and she got Squirrel a puppy. Do you remember Squirrel? The woman who used to hoard things excessively? But then our daughter, Ruth, was diagnosed with breast cancer, and she seemed to lose heart again – my wife, not Squirrel.' His conversation was really quite muddly.

'She took an overdose of paracetamol when I was away overnight and, when I found her, she was far past saving.'

'I'm sorry for your loss,' muttered Falconer, unable to think of anything else to say.

The mood was shattered by the creaking of the door, which had been left ajar, and by a quiet 'wuff'. A dachshund waddled into the room, immediately capturing Carmichael's attention, and he swooped off his chair and down to the floor to pet the dog.

'Say hello to Satan,' announced Rev. Ravenscastle. 'I don't know if you've met before, but he's my constant companion now, along with Captain Bligh, of course.'

'This little man is the reason I fell so in love with Dipsy Daxie,' explained Carmichael to anyone who would listen. He scratched the dog at the base of his tail, an action which was greeted with a contented sigh. Falconer rolled his eyes, remembering how his sergeant had taken on his own dachshund from the RSPCA after one of their recent cases.

He hadn't known how much Carmichael had been affected by his brief meeting with the vicar's dog. It explained a lot.

'Who or what is Dipsy Daxie?' The vicar was now confused.

'*My* dachshund,' replied the sergeant, a broad grin on his face as he petted the dog.

'Satan and I have something very important in common,' continued the vicar, no longer curious. 'We both wear dog collars – although we officially work for different sides, don't we, Satan old lad?'

The dog squinted up at his master with great affection as he extricated himself from Carmichael and waddled over to Ravenscastle's chair.

In an attempt to retrieve the situation, the inspector returned to the matter at hand and asked if the reverend could describe Ms Doidge to him. Ravenscastle closed his eyes briefly as if calling an image to mind, then spoke.

'She lived alone; had short brown hair; not married or divorced; no children. I think she was in her late twenties. King George III Terrace, if my memory serves me correctly. I did call round a couple of times after Perry and Tarquin said they couldn't get hold of her, but she certainly seemed to have left the property.'

Knowing he shouldn't ask, Falconer couldn't help himself from adding the question, 'How is your daughter, sir?'

'They didn't catch it early enough. It's spread, and she's terminal now. I visit her in a hospice every other day. She won't last much longer.'

How could one reply to that information? Falconer rose and said they'd see themselves out. As they reached the front door, the raucous screeching voice of the parrot called, 'Sod off,' after their retreating figures.

As they went back to the car, Falconer gave a great sigh, and said, 'How tragic was that? I had no idea what to say.'

'Me neither, sir,' agreed Carmichael, who hadn't really been paying attention, but wanted to sound as if he had taken in every detail.

'At least we know the woman's disappeared, too, or appears to have done. We'll have to look into it, but she sounds very similar to Annie Symons, doesn't she? Lives alone, single, quite young, not in any regular employment.'

'So where is she?' wondered Carmichael.

'And is she alive or dead?' mused Falconer. 'And we desperately need a photograph of her. When we get back to the office, I'll get Tomlinson to trace the owner and get a key, to see if there's anything inside the house that can help us.'

The inspector still felt uneasy about the chain of events that seemed to have been triggered by the death of Marcus Willoughby in Stoney Cross, including his own disturbing memories of Serena Lyddiard, and wondered if the ripples on the pond that ensued after any murder would ever end, or just keep resonating for the rest of the lifetimes of those involved.

That evening, Falconer took an inventory of his furry lodgers, calling their names out loud for reassurance. 'Tar Baby, Ruby!' – these were the two cats he'd taken on after his first love Serena had fled the country, a fluffy black monster and a

67

red-point Siamese. 'Mycroft!' – his first cat, a seal-point Siamese, slunk guiltily from beneath the sofa, and the inspector hoped he had not disturbed the dismemberment of a mouse or vole.

'Meep!' he called, for the Silver Bengal he had taken on from a rather intimidating lady and, finally, 'Monkey!' who had moved in on Carmichael as a stray, a tiny scrap full of mischief and independence, a pure bred Abyssinian.

Monkey appeared, coming down the stairs with a trail end of loo paper in her mouth, and he rushed up to where she had been, realising that he must have left the bathroom door open at lunchtime by mistake – a move that was always the precursor to a lot of mess to clear up. A sea of shredded toilet tissue greeted him but he was aware he could do nothing about it until he had collected a rubbish bag, and returned back downstairs to sort this out.

He heaved a sigh of relief that they were all present and correct as the cats milled around his legs in the kitchen. He opened the kitchen cupboard to get out a large tin of tuna – not that he wanted to bribe them into loving him, but just to say thank you for not running away, then he collected a black bag to clear up the mess in the bathroom.

Carmichael spent a quiet evening watching an episode of *Monk* that he had recorded, as Kerry had elected to go upstairs to bed early. As he had plenty of idiosyncrasies himself, Carmichael loved the antics of the American detective with OCD. Kerry, a deeply tired woman at the moment, had remembered nothing further about Annie Symons

68

and did not know Suzie Doidge, and had fallen straight to sleep with nothing nagging at her mind.

When Carmichael finally got upstairs, his wife was lying on her back fast asleep. A slight dribble of the white indigestion mixture she swigged nightly to combat the acid from which she suffered while pregnant every time she lay down, issued from a corner of her mouth.

As he sat on the bed to remove his shoes, she stirred and muttered a mild oath as she woke up.

'What's up?' he asked, concerned lest he should have disturbed her.

'These two, using my bladder as a trampoline,' she explained heading for the bathroom, but went straight back to sleep when she returned. As Carmichael was just dropping off he became aware of what sounded like a distant cheering and whistling, and got out of bed to look out of the window to see what on earth was going on in the village.

There was nobody abroad, and he returned to bed puzzled, until he listened carefully, and became aware that the noise was a sort of whistling snore coming from his wife's nostrils, something that never happened when she wasn't expecting. With a big grin over how he had been fooled, he went out like a light, sleeping the sleep of the righteous until the alarm went off.

Chapter Five

Just after nine the next morning, Tomlinson answered the phone to what sounded, to the other two occupants of the office, like a furious squawking. He handed the handset to Falconer, saying, 'Mr Jefferson Grammaticus, who won't speak to anyone but you. He's furious about something, but he won't tell me what.'

Falconer was surprised. Whatever did the owner of The Manse, a country hotel which was situated about seven miles to the east of Carsfold, want with him? Surely the man's ex-employee didn't want Meep back? he thought with a sudden jolt of panic. It was of course typical of him that his first thought should be for one of his cats.

'How can I help you, Mr Grammaticus?' he asked, taking the handset, the tiniest of wobbles in his voice.

'You can get down here and dig out the body that's just been discovered on my property!' the man bellowed. The owner of The Manse looked and sounded just like a country squire, and could be very abrupt in his manner.

'What body?'

'The one buried just beyond the confines of the drive.'

'I think you'd better explain further, Mr Grammaticus. You might know what's happened, but I don't.'

70

There was a pause, and then, 'Sorry, Falconer. Didn't think. I've had such success with my themed stays that I felt I needed to expand the guest car parking, but as the ground has been dug away to the sides, a body has appeared and, considering I paid for builders to be all over this site for the entire summer in 2010, I don't see how they could have done all that work and not found it.'

'I'll be over,' barked Falconer sharply, as he put the phone down and indicated to Carmichael to come with him. 'Tomlinson, you get on with trying to trace Suzie Doidge, and finding the contact numbers for the owners of 2 Drovers Lane and 7 King George III Terrace.'

They found the hotelier, his huge body quivering with indignation and clothed in very loud tweeds, out in the drive of the building, pacing back and forth like a caged lion. Without giving either of the detectives a chance of greeting him, the portly man burst out with, 'Will you look at this? Will you just look at this, and tell me what I'm going to do? I'm going to have a crime scene here, keeping out legitimate *and* potential customers, and it's going to go on for ages. I simply can't stand this sort of interruption to business, especially as things are going very well, now.'

He pointed down to part of a rib cage that had been uncovered when the site for the drive extension was being scraped by a digger. 'How the hell did that *not* get found when the work was done? And who the devil is it? I can't have corpses all over the place. This is a respectable establishment, you know.'

'Calm down, Mr Grammaticus. Perhaps we could go into your office and you could explain to me, slowly and carefully, how and when these remains were discovered, while DS Carmichael calls for officers to secure the site.' Falconer had a fleeting thought that this could be their missing Suzie Doidge, and thought how tidy and convenient that would be. Yes, they'd still have to find the killer, but if this wasn't that woman from Stoney Cross, then they had a fourth dead or missing person to deal with. Then this could become the case of a serial killer at work, and that was something he couldn't even imagine dealing with.

Grammaticus took a deep breath before starting his explanation. 'I got the men in to expand the parking area, and I'm enjoying great success by doing themed breaks.' He had originally aimed at doing something much more classy – 'I forgot all that nonsense about making it a six-star experience after those murders, and I've never looked back. People love play-acting, and we're making a bomb, hence the parking.'

'But when the digger started to take off the top layer they came across those ribs, and there's obviously the rest of a body down there. Actually, it looks like the digger may have disturbed the decaying flesh, because from what I can see, the rest of it seems to have flesh of some sort over it. God, how gruesome.'

'When did this come to light?'

'First thing this morning and I rang you, straight away, as soon as I knew it wasn't some sort of practical joke.'

72

'Why would you think that?'

'There are some weird folk around, and it could have been a delaying tactic from the opposition.'

'Which opposition?'

'Other hotel owners who are jealous of my success.'

Yeah, right! 'I don't think so. So, let's assume that this body was there before the workmen did the work back in 2010. Why would they not have come across it? It looks to be right on the edge of the drive to me. What if the body was put there later? Is there any possibility of that? I'm sure they'd have found it when they carried out the initial digging if it had already been there.'

'I suppose so,' Grammaticus conceded, 'but who the hell's put it there, and was it when the drive was first laid, or later?'

'That's what we need to find out, along with who it is, and who killed them.'

'Look, Inspector, I simply *can't* have a crime scene here. It's unthinkable.'

'It's right on the edge of your parking area. Don't you think it might add to the atmosphere if you have a crime-themed gathering?' Falconer played to the man's weak point: namely, his back pocket.

'I hadn't thought of that. Good thinking, man!' Jefferson Grammaticus positively beamed at them at this ingenious suggestion. 'In that case, it's not so bad. We've actually got a murder weekend at the end of this week – I can turn a profit from this!'

'I'll have to send a crime scene investigation team over to examine the area. When they've reported back to me, and we've had a chance to see if anyone's missing, I'll get in touch with you again with any information we may have gathered. Carmichael, you can put your notebook away now.'

Carmichael had noted down this last statement before he realised it was directed at him, and looked up in surprise. Was this all? He supposed there was little they could do for the present and the body had not appeared there overnight, so looking at the guests currently staying at the establishment would not really be of any use to them.

'I've still got that cat, you know?' Falconer suddenly blurted out.

'What cat, Inspector? Have you taken leave of your senses?'

'The one that belonged to your former housekeeper, Beatrix Ironmonger,' he replied with some dignity. 'She called her Perfect Cadence. A silver-spotted Bengal.'

'Did she? I don't even remember her having a cat, but I knew she liked them. And you took it in, did you? Very kind of you, I'm sure.' Falconer fairly bristled at this lapse of memory on the part of Grammaticus.

'And she's very well cared for,' put in Carmichael, 'with lots of brothers and sisters.' This was a fairly inaccurate statement, but he couldn't let the occasion pass without making comment in Falconer's defence.

'Very nice, I'm sure. Now, I must get on. I've got a murder to organise, and now I know there has to be a body under the drive.' The hotelier rose, to indicate that the interview was over, now he had worked out how to manipulate events to his advantage, and the two detectives made their way back outside. As they left the office the

74

hotelier was running his hands over his facial hair with glee at this unforeseen profit-making opportunity, and grinning triumphantly.

'What a chancer!' declared Falconer, when they were once more in the open air and out of earshot.

'A right modern-day spiv, if you ask me, sir,' concurred his sergeant.

'You're far too young to know about spivs.'

'I've seen the St Trinian's films, haven't I, sir?'

'Of course you have, Carmichael. Of course you have.'

'He hasn't mellowed at all, has he?'

'Not a jot, Sergeant.'

Tomlinson, meanwhile, took a jaunt out to Castle Farthing, this being one of the many villages that he hadn't visited yet. He knew Market Darley quite well, but the smaller communities he had only been to when a case had dictated he go there. Surprised by its photogenic good looks, he readily located Drovers Lane after taking a short stroll round the green.

Having brought with him printed notes asking the occupants to contact him, with his office and mobile numbers on it, he pushed them through the letterboxes of numbers three, six, seven, and eight. He then sat down on one of the benches on the green to phone his partner, Imogen. She had promised to be there tonight when he got home from work, and he was eager to confirm this promise. He could never be sure of his hours, working in the police service, and Imi worked in hospitality, on a shift system at one of the local hotels, where she dealt with bookings and events and made sure the phones were manned at all times.

Tomlinson punched a fist into the air in triumph, as he sat in the weak sunshine, when Imi confirmed that they would be able to spend the evening together, and he just hoped that Falconer wouldn't find him something to do after his hours ended. If the occupants of Drovers Lane did contact him he could arrange to meet them the next day, but he didn't fancy losing his cosy evening in front of the television curled up with his beloved. In his innocence, he had no idea how complicated his work life was about to become. This transfer had seemed like a good plan, to a small town with surrounding sleepy villages. How naïve.

Meanwhile, a CSI team had been dispatched to The Manse, and Doc Christmas invited along to confirm that death had, indeed, occurred – a ridiculous procedure, but a necessary one to work by the book.

The medical man looked at the remains that had been uncovered on the very edge of the gravelled drive and sighed. That digger had certainly made a mess of the front of the body, but then it was a heavy machine with a lot of power behind the bucket. How long had this one been there? He wondered idly, before kneeling down to examine it more closely. It certainly wasn't as fresh as a daisy, that was for sure. It was still quite early in the day, though, and if he could get it lifted, he could get it on to his post-mortem table before knocking off time.

The team worked around him, photographing, filming, taking soil samples, and looking for any clues that the surrounding earth could yield.

Christmas's mind went back to the body of the first woman that had been discovered. He had identified nick marks on three of her ribs, indicating that she had been stabbed in the chest. This one seemed to have had her throat cut.

It may have been a different method of murder, but it still involved a knife, and he wondered if the two young women – for such was this as well – could have been killed by the same person, and how much time there had been between the two deaths.

A gut feeling told him there was over a year between these two killings, but he'd see what he could uncover later in the pathology suite. He would conclude that the victim had been in her late twenties to early thirties, and that she had been placed in the ad hoc grave somewhere in the summer of 2010...

When Falconer and Carmichael got back to the office Doc Christmas had left messages with the details about methods of dispatch concerning both murders, and Tomlinson arrived back just after them. Falconer sat behind his desk with his head in his hands. 'This looks like it's going to be a nasty one, gentlemen. We've got two bodies now, and neither of them buried themselves. Is this one going to prove to be our Suzie Doidge? Tomlinson, can you do your trick with the dentists again? There's no jewellery to help with the identity this time. I don't want to disturb Ms Warwick again saying we might have found her friend, and then have to tell her that we haven't.

'Right, the sergeant and I will go to speak to the

neighbours in King George III Terrace, see what we can find out about Suzie Doidge. Tomlinson, have you traced the owners of number seven, and two Drovers Lane, so that we can find out what they know about their previous tenants?'

At that point Falconer's phone rang, obliterating Tomlinson's comment that he hadn't had any luck yet, and he found Bob Bryant, the desk sergeant, on the other end. 'We've got a woman in here who says that her daughter's gone missing. I wondered if you could have a chat with her.' With a sigh at the thought of another disappearance, the inspector rose and plodded downstairs with an air of concern about how many more young women might disappear if they had a serial kidnapper and killer on their hands.

In interview room one he confronted a very distressed woman weeping into a sodden tissue. She looked at him with drowned eyes, and wailed, 'You've got to find my Natalie! She didn't come back the night before last; she didn't come home or contact us yesterday and her phone's just going to her answering service. I think it's turned off. She was only going out for a drink, and she just never came home, and I'm so worried about her.'

'Has she ever done anything like this before?' asked Falconer, drawing out a small notebook from his jacket pocket.

'Never. She always lets me know where she is, who she's with, and what she's doing.'

Although Falconer didn't believe this was necessarily true, he carried on with his questions. 'How old is Natalie? Have you got a photograph of her?'

'Right here in my handbag,' replied the woman,

fumbling around inside the bag. 'She's twenty-two, and she doesn't go out a lot. I can't imagine where she is and why she hasn't contacted me.'

Falconer took the proffered snapshot and saw a picture of a young woman with bright blue eyes and long, wavy blonde hair. 'Does she have a boyfriend?' This often solved a lot of missing person reports concerning young females.

'No. She's a bit shy and doesn't mix much.'

'And yet she went out for a drink. With whom?'

'I don't really know. She just said she was meeting someone, but I'm so worried about her.'

'Has she, to your knowledge, been associating with anyone lately that you don't approve of?'

'She has very few friends, mainly on that book-face computer thingy, and this is just so unlike her.'

'Where does she work, if she does, and may I have her mobile number and details of your address and home contact numbers?'

After checking exactly when she had last seen her daughter, he asked her if she had noticed if she'd taken anything from her bedroom: underwear, toiletries, make-up, but the answer was in the negative. He was given a pretty clear picture of a fairly solitary twenty-two year old who mixed little and worked quietly, without having a wild social life with her colleagues. She sounded a very lonely young woman, apart from 'that book-face thingy'.

The interview ground to its inevitable end, the inspector promising that he'd get Natalie's photograph circulated and get all available officers to look out for her. He'd also check the hospitals, but

79

she must promise to telephone if Natalie got in touch at all.

When he returned to his office he instructed Tomlinson to phone the hospitals in the greater Carsfold area, and get the photo copied to all officers, before grabbing Carmichael for their second visit in two days to Stoney Cross. 'Come on, Carmichael,' he exhorted, without another thought. 'It's time to get back to Stoney Cross, see what we can discover about Ms Doidge. Tomlinson, you carry on checking the hospitals, and see what you can dig up using your very useful dentists again.'

With a sigh of resignation, the DC picked up the phone and began to punch in numbers.

It would turn out that he hadn't taken the supposed disappearance of Natalie Jones seriously enough.

Chapter Six

King George III Terrace was a long row of houses built with basements, so there were steps up to each main door. Number seven had two occupants, but the ground floor flat was empty. It had not been re-let, which was rather odd.

The occupant of the first-floor flat turned out to have a key, which she had almost forgotten about, finally fishing it out of a drawer of odds and ends in her kitchenette, and she let them into the place. This was fortunate as Falconer had the dreadful sinking feeling that he was going to have to use his extremely poor lock-picking talents to gain entry. After a quick look inside, the woman from the flat above bowed out and left them to it.

The flat didn't seem to have been cleared out after the tenant went missing, and this was surprising. Although she had not been reported missing they thought the landlord would have picked up on the fact that she was no longer there, and would have moved the woman's possessions out, so that he could re-let it. Falconer made a mental note to check with the two women's banks to make sure that the rent hadn't just gone on being paid. Although 2 Drovers Lane had new tenants, he wondered how long it had been since Suzie Doidge disappeared that the owner found out about it, and whether he had stopped the regular monthly income into his account.

The flat itself was in an appalling state, not only extremely untidy and dusty, but also in desperate need of some work being done on it. The kitchen and bathroom fittings were ancient, the carpet almost threadbare, and the whole place desperately needed a coat of paint. No wonder Ms Doidge didn't do anything in it: it must have been a very disheartening place to live.

'What is that ghastly smell?' asked Falconer, wrinkling his nose.

'I think it's coming from the drains,' replied Carmichael. 'The water hasn't been run for a very long time, and if the access points dry out you can get a very foul stench coming up.'

Falconer watched, fascinated, as his sergeant turned on every tap in the place and then flushed the lavatory. 'That should help a bit. Here, sir, I'll open a window to freshen the place up.'

The fridge proved to be full of dried-out rotten food, the wall cupboard with out-of-date, dusty packets and tins. Even the kitchen waste bin hadn't been emptied, its decomposed contents still lining the bottom of the receptacle. The towels in the bathroom still bore a faint dried crust of mould where they hadn't had the chance to dry out after the place had been left to rot, and there were old magazines and junk mail everywhere.

'God, what a dump!' exclaimed the inspector. 'Not house-proud, was she?'

'Maybe she expected to come back to it,' suggested Carmichael, with eminent common sense. 'She'd not have known she was going to disappear off the face of the earth. A lot of people living on their own only have a real good go at their home once a week.'

Falconer had to give in to this logical thinking, facing up to the fact that everyone wasn't so fastidious as he was, and suggested that they started looking round for an address book or diary, either of which would help them with people who knew the previous occupant.

In an overflowing sideboard they found several old diaries, a few colour photographs which depicted a woman of about the right age and description as Ms Doidge, and an ancient address book; which Falconer bagged ready to be looked through for clues to the woman's life, whom she might have known, and whom she might have seen on the last night of her existence.

He assumed she was dead. It seemed after all unreasonable that she would just have run off and never contacted anyone again. Not that they might not find a number of people, perhaps noted in the address book, who knew perfectly well where she was, and had had no idea that she'd just evaporated into thin air as far as her employers and neighbour were concerned.

'Let's have a word with the woman upstairs, see how well she knew Ms Doidge,' suggested Falconer. 'Maybe the woman's alive and well and living and working in Aylesbury, Aberystwyth, or Aberdeen, and just left here rather suddenly as a result of something that happened immediately before she left.'

'Unlikely, sir, as she doesn't seem to have collected any of her personal possessions. The wardrobe's full of clothes, the dressing table's covered with make-up and perfume, and there's even some stuff in a laundry basket waiting to be washed.'

'You're right, of course. I can see someone flouncing off in a huge huff, but I can't see them never collecting all their worldly goods, though, can you?'

'Unlikely, sir.'

On the first floor the woman asked them in, introduced herself as Jasmine Giles, and offered tea or coffee. Carmichael accepted with a smile, saying, 'My house is called Jasmine too – Jasmine Cottage!' Falconer looked around him at the first-floor flat. Although in a similar state of lack of maintenance and disrepair, everything in it was immaculate and there was no mess whatsoever. The vintage of the furnishings, however, was 'early jumble-sale', the sofa and chairs' outdated chintz jazzed up with a history of mysterious stains that could have told a very long and interesting story. The sideboard was the sort of 1930s relic that would never attract a high price as a 'period piece' at auction.

Seeing him looking, Miss Giles, who asked them to call her Jasmine, said, 'Both flats are in a bit of a state, neglected, like, and the basement's only used for junk, but the rent's low, and it suits me at the moment to put away as much as I can from my wages. I'm saving up to go travelling.'

'Why don't you get the landlord to do something?' asked Carmichael, who was soft-hearted and had just noticed the large brown stains on the ceiling which suggested that the roof was not in good order.

'He lives abroad, and he's really not interested. And it suits my thinking at the moment. If he refurbished these places, he'd charge more rent, and I'm happy as I am. I'll soon be off to the Far East and Australia, and I want as much in my bank account as possible.'

'Do you have an address or contact details for him?'

'Somewhere; I'll just have a look for you. I remember he had some estimates done when Suzie was here, and he didn't like the figure that was suggested to put the flats into good order.'

'What did Ms Doidge think of the state of the place?'

'She didn't really care. All she wanted was new clothes and to go out. She just wanted to meet someone special and settle down. She always said that one day her prince would come.'

'But she'd surely not bring him back here?' Fal-

84

coner had spoken without thinking, and he felt embarrassed that he could have hurt Jasmine's feelings. 'I'm sorry, I didn't mean that like it sounded.'

'No offence taken. As I've just explained, I have a reason for living in a dump like this, and so did Suzie. She didn't have a lot of hours' work a week, and she was on a really limited budget. For all her love of clothes, she had to manage to find fancy stuff in charity shops at minimal prices. And when she went out, she expected to find some man and lure him into buying all her drinks.'

'I understand that she was also claiming benefits?' the inspector asked.

'Only what she was entitled to in Working Tax Credits,' Jasmine replied. 'She never claimed anything that she wasn't due. She wasn't like that. She may have lived in a rat's nest but she was a romantic, and very honest.'

'When did you last see her?' asked Falconer.

'It must have been a couple of years ago, now I come to think about it. I just assumed she had gone off with someone.'

'Did you know her well?'

'We weren't that close, but sometimes she used to come up for a coffee or a glass of wine at my place.'

'Do you know if she had a boyfriend; a regular one?'

'Now you mention it, there was someone she was going to see, but she didn't want to talk about it much, which wasn't like her at all. And it was someone new, as far as I know.'

'So she didn't tell you who it was?'

'No. She was rather secretive about it, but said she'd tell me all when she could, which was very mysterious.'

'Did she have a lot of boyfriends?'

'Quite a lot. As I said, she was always looking for Mr Right, and coming up with Mr Left or Mr Wrong.'

'Do you remember any of their names?'

'She wasn't usually with them long enough to ask them back for coffee, so she hardly ever brought anyone home. No, I can't remember any names. She didn't exactly introduce me if she came home with someone on whom she had evil designs – sexual ones, I mean. And the ones she did bring back here she never stayed with long. I suppose they didn't measure up to her exacting demands.'

This last comment made the woman blush, but she merely cleared her throat and didn't add anything to it.

'Right, Miss Giles – Jasmine – I think that'll be all for now, if you'll just get those contact details for us and write down your own phone number, we'll be off.' Falconer waited for Carmichael to stop scribbling in his notebook, and stood, preparatory to leaving. 'If you remember anything else that may be useful to us, please contact us at Market Darley Police Station. Here's my card, and I'm sure DS Carmichael has one for you, too.'

'I will, but it all seems so long ago.'

'It is,' concurred Carmichael, wondering how on earth they were going to find this woman.

Back at the station, Tomlinson had had no luck

with the hospitals in his search for Natalie Jones – but had he struck gold, or even ceramic, when he contacted the dentist who had come up with the first victim's identity? Not this time – but he had, however, experienced more luck with a different dental practitioner, who came up with the name Melanie Saunders and an address in Carsfold. He had also managed to trace the landlord who owned 2 Drovers Lane, and handed all the information over to the inspector to do with what he wished.

'That's *another* one,' said Falconer in despair. 'I thought it was going to be Suzie Doidge, and it turns out to be someone else altogether. That's two dead, and two missing. What's been going on in this area over the last few years? It seems like we've got a serial killer, if all these things are related. And in that case where the hell is Suzie Doidge – or at least her remains? And how the hell has he slipped under the radar for so long, completely undetected and unsuspected? We have no more clue to the killer's identity than we had when you stumbled over that first body in the woods. It's like he's invisible.

'Carmichael, can you phone these two people – they're the owners of the two properties where our first two missing women lived, and see what you can get out of them about their previous tenants. Also, get on to the women's banks and see if, or when, their rent stopped being paid automatically. For all we know, these two ruthless landlords are still extracting money from the dead. The question is, do they know what they're doing, or might be doing? And if the rents stopped, why didn't they try to re-let the properties?' Falconer stumbled to a halt, realising that he was reacting in panic to this further supposedly disappeared and/or murdered woman.

'Strike that. That's something that I'll deal with myself: the landlords, at least. Carmichael, you check with the banks in town to see where they had their accounts if we don't already have the information, I'll,' here he took his scrap of paper back, 'talk to these two ruthless property tycoons.

'OK, Tomlinson, now see if you can trace where Ms Saunders worked, and any other details about her life that may help us to find out why she ended up where she did.' That was all three of them taken care of. He didn't, however, rank Natalie Jones in his calculations. He was fairly sure she'd soon be home with her tail between her legs and a secret smile on her face.

The owner of 2 Drovers Lane sounded like a decent man on the phone and arranged to meet Falconer in thirty minutes in Café Figaro to tell him his side of the story. The owner of the King George III Terrace property was apparently currently resident in France, according to his tenant Jasmine Giles. He claimed to have had no idea that his tenant was missing and admitted that, yes, he had been a bit lax in inspecting the place, but that he didn't like to employ a managing agent because of the extra expense. It wasn't as if the flats were expensive to rent. He'd stop the payment immediately and was very sorry for his error.

Yes, thought the inspector with a disapproving frown. And pigs might fly. And they hadn't found anyone who would take the time and effort to claim back the money, either. This woman seemed to have no relatives.

Thirty minutes later saw him in Café Figaro with a Mr Bridger. The man looked very benevolent, was about retirement age and sported a rather natty and thick moustache and beard. 'I'm very distressed to hear that my previous tenant in Castle Farthing has been found, um, ah, deceased. I've only just heard the news on the local radio. I realised, when I went round to inspect the decorating, about a month after the man went in to carry out the work, that there didn't seem to be anybody there. I carried on visiting in the hope that, if my tenant was out, I'd catch her in at a different time, on a different day of the week.'

'As time went on, though, I realised that she'd just left the place, especially when I looked through the kitchen window at the back, and could see the same mug on the table, and the same knife and plate on the draining board. I stopped the payments of rent the next day. It didn't seem fair to take money that was not officially owed to me.

'I simply can't believe that she was dead all that time. My wife, Pauline, will be absolutely horrified when I tell her. I thought she'd just moved on and been too remiss to let me know.'

The man's explanation sounded sincere, and Falconer accepted it at face value. What point would there be in lying, especially as he had Carmichael checking the bank account? So, so far, it didn't seem that either landlord was involved with either of the first two disappearances. But what about this third woman whose body had been found at The Manse?

Falconer shooed the other two detectives off home on time that night, and left the office himself unusually early. When he got to his house his eye was taken by the bird feeder he had purchased the previous weekend and hung out only the night before, full of seed. This interest in the welfare of wild birds was a new hobby for him, and he was amazed that the receptacle was already empty.

Greedy little gits, he thought, as he unhooked it from the tree branch and carried it indoors. He had decided to place it outside the front of the house so that the cats would not be enticed by birds gathering at it. He had once had a bird table in a tree in the back garden, and two days after he had put it up, came out to find one of his furry charges sitting on it, practically with his mouth open – the new feeder was his compromise.

After refilling it on going back into the house, he was aware that, whereas all the cats were usually there to greet him, tonight, there was one missing. Where had Monkey got to? She was one that was unfailingly there to welcome him.

He had a quick look in the back garden, then upstairs in the bedrooms and bathroom. No, no cat under his bed, no cat in the bathroom playing with the loo roll, and no cat in his laundry basket catching a quick snooze. There was no sign of her. Slipping back outside into the darkness, he called her, but elicited no response. That was odd.

He was rather distracted while he threw together something for his evening meal. As he washed up the few dishes he'd dirtied in his culinary efforts there was a ring at the front doorbell, and he wondered who would be calling on him unexpectedly in the evening.

On the doorstep stood Honey, all smiles. 'What are we eating?' she asked, working her way past him and into the house. He merely stood where he was, a look of mingled amazement and horror on his face.

'What day is it?' he asked.

'Don't you remember, you asked me to come round for a bite to eat tonight? And don't worry that I'll start throwing cats around, jump on your sofa and scream my head off. I really am cured.' A multiple clacking of the cat-flap showed that his pets did not have the same confidence in her, and had exited at the first sound of her voice.

'Oh, God, I'm so sorry. I completely forgot it was today, and I've already eaten.'

'What are you like? Completely married to the job!'

The word 'married' shot through him like a crossbow bolt, and he had to pull himself together. She hadn't meant anything by that. 'Come on in,' he said, somewhat after the event, 'and I'll rustle something up for you.'

'Don't worry. I'll order a pizza or something to be delivered. Are you sure you're OK for me to be here? You seem somewhat distracted.'

'We've got a lot on at the moment: two young women confirmed dead and two missing, and Monkey doesn't seem to be around. I know she's only a cat and I can't expect her to be here to meet me home from work every day, but the fact is, she usually does, and it doesn't seem right that she's not here.'

'I'll come back another night. I can see you're not going to be very good company this evening. No, don't worry about it. I can always find something to do,' replied Honey, thinking that he seemed just as concerned about his pet as he was about the deaths and disappearances – but he was a somewhat odd man, and she'd just have to get used to that.

Falconer, still not really aware of his social faux pas and bad manners, closed the door in a distracted manner, and went out into the back garden again to call, 'Monkey! Monkey, where are you?' making little kissing noises to try to distract her from whatever she was involved in and attract her home.

Chapter Seven

Monkey had not arrived back the next morning when Falconer got up, but he had awoken with a very uneasy feeling which didn't take too long to identify itself. He'd been appallingly off-hand with Honey – which was probably partly to do with his guilt over thinking of Serena Lyddiard so often in the recent past – but was deeply unnerved by how the thought of marriage had disturbed him. Still, the most important problem on his mind was the little cat, and he wondered if his second try with Honey was a good idea. He had been so hurt by her the first time around, and he didn't think his anger had really gone away. Maybe the whole

92

thing was a mistake.

Why should he be so much more worried about a little Abyssinian cat than he was about having totally forgotten that the love of his life (or, at least, she whom he had previously considered thus) had been coming round? And then to dismiss her when she did show up! Why did he keep thinking of Serena? And why wasn't he able to give his all to the case?

He needed to sort out his thoughts about his relationship with Honey Dubois, and evaluate if he could ever totally forgive her for what she had done when she had been back to her home island. But where *had* his little cat got to? Was she in a gutter somewhere, beyond recognition, or had she been enticed into someone's car? Monkey was a very sociable little thing, and he wanted her back.

Resolving to walk the local streets in search of her, he steeled himself to finding her tiny, broken body, and left the house without breakfast or even a cup of coffee. Had he smoked, he would have lit up before he went out: sometimes he wished he had that vice and comfort to lean on in times of stress.

Later, he would print out a photograph of the cat with a message with his phone number on it and stick it on to lampposts and telegraph poles in the area, and call into the local shops. If she was out there, alive or dead, he would resolve the mystery, just to put his mind at rest about her fate.

He arrived at his office somewhat later than usual, and Carmichael and Tomlinson were already at their desks, but there was something odd about

93

Carmichael. He squinted at him and asked, 'Sergeant, why has your hair got green strands in the front?'

'Sorry, sir. I've been trying to get it out.' Carmichael looked more than sheepish.

'Gum again?'

'A huge bubble. It burst.'

'Evidently. Go to the canteen and see if they'll give you some ice. If you put that over it, it should freeze it so that you can remove it.'

'Thank you, sir. I'll remember that one,' said the sergeant rising from his chair.

'Of course, if you never chew it again in my sight, this won't recur.'

'Sorry, sir. Won't happen again.'

'Good! Promise?'

The office door closed behind Carmichael's retreating figure before he could make this all-important agreement.

Falconer was just getting settled when his internal phone rang, and he answered it to hear the voice of Superintendent Chivers on the line.

'Falconer? My office. Now.'

Chivers didn't waste words. The inspector's face blanched, and he told Tomlinson he'd be back as soon as he could. Suddenly a sergeant chewing gum didn't seem so important.

Chivers' office was always immaculately tidy, and had a wall full of bookshelves lined with weighty legal volumes. The carpet was thick and luxurious, and the superintendent always looked as if his wife had freshly ironed him every morning straight after breakfast.

'Sit down, Inspector, and tell me what the hell's

going on?' he barked. 'I've had a call from one of my wife's friends to say she came in here yesterday to report her daughter missing, and you don't seem to have done anything about it.'

'What?'

'Mrs Ida Jones came in to report her daughter Natalie missing. She was expecting someone to call round and take more details before starting a search for her, and yet she's heard nothing since she visited the station. Why are you sitting on your thumbs, man? You're a policeman, not a solicitor. We've already got two young women dead, and now we've got one missing.'

Suddenly catching the drift, Falconer responded with, 'Actually we've got two missing. The second body turned out to be someone else, and we still don't know what happened to Suzie Doidge.'

'Dear God, that's even worse than I thought. Why have you been so inactive?'

'I thought, as her mother said that Natalie was a rather shy girl, that maybe she'd met someone of, er, the opposite gender, and been too scared to let her mother know she wasn't coming home. I thought she'd probably met a man and had gone off with him somewhere, and that she'd turn up yesterday evening looking sheepish.'

'You did, did you? And did she?'

'Not to my knowledge, sir.'

'Not to anyone else's knowledge, either. You should be ashamed of yourself for taking the whole thing so lightly. Now, I'll tell you what I'm going to do, I'm going to make a TV appeal for this girl, Natalie Jones, and put out details for the other one who hasn't turned up. I want her details, along with those for the dead girls, on my desk as soon as is humanly possible. If we're not competent or interested enough to find out what's been going on then we shall have to rely on the public to do our job for us, Inspector. What do you have to say about that?'

Falconer gulped at this furious attack.

'And I hope you're ashamed of yourself. Maybe you'd be better employed looking after a pack of Brownies as their Brown Owl. You certainly don't seem mature and responsible, or even interested enough, to handle a complicated case like this one.'

'No, sir.'

'Is that all you've got to say for yourself?'

'I'll have the information we have collected up here as soon as possible, and I'll pay more attention to detail in future. We've only just got a name for the second body, but we have traced the owners of the properties that the two who first went missing lived in. I've already contacted the landlords, and I've put DC Tomlinson on to tracing where the latest victim lived and worked to see if we can unearth any contacts.'

'Go on then, Inspector, get to it. Don't stand around in my office gawping at me all day long. And let me make this clear: I will *not* have my wife taking calls from members of the public, even if it *is* an acquaintance of hers, making *complaints* about the *inefficiency* of my officers. I will *not* be made a fool of in *my own town.*' By the time he finished shouting, his face was engorged with rage and there was spittle at the corners of his mouth.

Falconer replied in a raised voice, 'No, sir!' and

had to restrain his impulse to salute. He knew he was not running at full capacity, and resolved to do something about it.

On his trip back down the stairs he resolved to pull himself together. He would send Carmichael to go through the boxes again that Rosemary Wilson had stored in her stock room in the shop at Castle Farthing, and get Tomlinson to gather any information that he could on Melanie Saunders. Chivers would sort out the TV appeal for Natalie Jones – he did so like being the centre of media attention – then he could get on with organising a search, if necessary. The girl could still be alive, although she definitely wasn't in hospital after an accident.

He needed to know where she had been the evening she disappeared, and hoped that the information would come in after Chivers' appearance on the local news. It was certainly more likely that people would remember seeing her than they would the two who had worked behind the bar at The Inn on the Green and The Fisherman's Flies on an ad hoc basis so long ago. The public memory wasn't as long as he would have liked it to be.

Tomlinson got straight on to his computer and the phone, while Carmichael grabbed his coat to drive back to Castle Farthing, from whence he had recently arrived. He was glad of the chance to get back to his home village as Kerry had been suffering from lower back pain the previous evening and was extremely uncomfortable, physically. He could call in to see how she was before returning to the office.

Mrs Wilson greeted Carmichael with a wide smile and asked him what he wanted. When he explained the purpose of his visit, she immediately showed him into the back of the shop and pointed again at the boxes that held Annie Symons' possessions. 'Any idea what you're looking for, Davey?' she asked him. 'You've already had a riffle through them once.'

'More photographs, an address book or a diary,' he replied, making a stab at what Falconer expected of him. 'Anything, really, that will give us clues to anyone she might have known. I've spoken to Kerry, but she didn't know her all that well.'

'Did you trace that cousin in Australia?' the shopkeeper asked.

'We don't even have a name, yet.'

'Well, good luck. She wasn't a very chatty person, but she might have written things down.'

Carmichael must have had a bit of the Irish in him that day. Under a flap in the bottom of the box he came across a first draft of a children's book that the young woman had been putting together, along with some fairly naïve illustrations, and an address book that listed several numbers he thought might be connected to this literary attempt. That should give them something to work on.

He also located a few more photographs that he thought looked fairly recent given that the little Jack Russell, Buster, who used to belong to the miserly old curmudgeon who had lived in the right-hand half of what was now his and Kerry's home, was in the background. She was sitting on

98

the little wall at the front of her cottage with another young woman, whom he presumed to be a friend, and the photo must have been taken by a third party.

After loading the whole lot into his car, in the hope that there would be something else of use to them in it after it had been sifted through thoroughly, he called briefly on Kerry and found her feeling very poorly. He had to promise to come home on time, if not early, that evening so that she could get some rest. Harriet was running her ragged now she was on two feet, and his wife was clearly exhausted with her large size.

When he returned to his desk, Falconer grabbed the photographs, and ran them straight up to the superintendent's office. He was planning to film the appeal for the lunchtime bulletin, and so far this was the only further pictorial evidence of Annie Symons.

He found his superior combing his hair in front of a wall mirror; he was practising looking serious and concerned. His brisk rap on the door and entry without waiting to be summoned in must have embarrassed Chivers, because his face was red when he turned round to receive this necessary evidence of the dead woman's appearance.

'I'll put that with the other things you brought me earlier, Inspector. See what you can find on that other woman, Saunders, and get to grips with Natalie's disappearance, there's a good man.' It was amazing what a bit of being caught out preening could do to a person's attitude.

When he got back Tomlinson had discovered from the electoral register where Ms Saunders had lived, and gone out to pay a visit to the address, and Carmichael was bursting with conflicting emotions. The most personal one reared its head first. 'Can I get away fairly swiftly today, sir? Kerry's feeling very low and I want her to be able to have a nice long soak and an early night. All this extra weight is taking its toll on her.

'Oh, and I've remembered something from when we worked on a murder case in Shepford Stacey. There was a house at the end of a road where the occupant had suddenly disappeared. I'll have a look through my old notebooks and see if I can come across her name, but it might be another one of these disappearances.'

'I seem to remember something about that. You sort out a name and I'll follow it up. And, as to your going home early, I don't really think so, with so much to be investigated, but I certainly won't keep you late. If anything happens to Kerry, you'll miss a lot more work than if I let you go and look after her.'

'Thank you, sir. I'll go and hunt out that old notebook straight away.'

While he was gone, Falconer could hear the sound of feet on stone steps and the inane chatter of a crowd of reporters, all intent on a good story so that maybe, just this once, they could shout, 'Hold the front page'. He heard the babble enter the building and head for the conference room where, no doubt, 'Jelly' Chivers was preening himself for the approaching publicity: yet another chance to have his likeness beamed into innumerable homes and directly to address *his* public. Sometimes he took his role as public protector

100

seriously, at others, he just wanted to lick the boots of more senior officers in the hope of some house points and the possibility of promotion.

Boy was he going to be smug after this, with other senior officers phoning him to congratulate him on his handling of the media – or at least the superintendent hoped that was how it was going to be, and that he wouldn't goof-up, make a laughing stock of himself, and end up with egg all over his face.

Carmichael returned to the office half an hour later with an expression of triumph on his face. 'Fanny Anstruther,' he announced. 'Copse View on Blacksmiths Terrace. It was assumed that she'd gone into a nursing home, but nobody knew for certain. Do you want me to follow it up?'

'Did you find out who'd told us that it was thought she'd gone into a home?'

'The vicar's wife, Ruth Lockwood, sir.'

'I'll give her a ring and ask her what she remembers about the house and woman. Her number should be easy enough to find if she's married to the vicar, although I've probably got it on file somewhere.'

Before he could pick up the phone, however, it rang and he found Tomlinson on the line. 'I'm in Carsfold at the address we had for Melanie Saunders, and I've spoken to the neighbours. They said she had an interview through an employment agency for a job as a live-in just before she went away. They just assumed she'd taken the job and moved, although they couldn't recall her moving her stuff out – but as both of them work, they thought she could easily have picked up her pos-

101

sessions while they were out. What do you want me to do next, sir?'

'Give the agency a visit, Tomlinson, and well done. If we can find out where and when the interview was, we can at least get an approximate time for her disappearance.'

'Will do. It's in Market Darley, so I'll come straight back and let you know if I've got anything.'

As he ended the call, Falconer could hear the sound of chairs being scraped in the conference room, prior to being stacked and stored along the back wall, and he knew he would soon hear the sound of Chivers' feet trotting up the stairs after his moment in the limelight. A moment of unintended schadenfreude had him hoping that the man had made a fool of himself and been ambushed by a barrage of unexpected questions for which he hadn't rehearsed, but this passed quickly, as he didn't want to think that the case had been hindered by his superior's handling of the press.

Before he had time to think of anything else, the phone rang again, and he found Honey on the line.

'I was just following up from last night. When do you want us to meet again?' Now, this was a reasonable question, considering how their relationship had been going, but Falconer was thoroughly unsettled, and had momentarily forgotten his contrition of the morning. He reacted to a gut instinct.

'I don't think we should see each other for a while. I've got a very complicated case at work which is going to occupy the whole of my thoughts for some time. Maybe we could just cool our relationship off a little. Just until things are more under control. Only for a short time. Not very long...' His words died in his mouth.

As he spoke, he listened to his statements as if they were the ramblings of a stranger, but knew that he was doing the right thing. Work was going to take all his time until this case was wound up, and the misgivings he had been experiencing suddenly solidified in his head. He wasn't as happy as he'd thought he was. He still couldn't entirely forgive this lovely woman, nor could he forget about her infidelity ... it would be best if he didn't see her for a while. Maybe it would be for the best if he didn't see her at all, if he was more concerned with the disappearance of his pet than he was about upsetting his girlfriend, but he wasn't going to say that just at the moment. Better not burn a bridge until he knew whether he'd have to cross it again.

'I'll ring again in a couple of weeks,' responded Honey, with a chirpy note in her voice, not giving in that easily. 'I'll just keep my eyes on the local news and work out when everything's in hand. OK?'

'No problem.' Why had he said that? His over-cautious side exerting itself, again?

He left the office for an early lunch, leaving the contacting of Ruth Lockwood to later. He'd nip home and see if Monkey had reappeared, thinking he had no idea how badly he'd react if it was a family member who had seemed to disappear off the face of the earth if he felt this way about a cat.

And what was wrong with him with regard to Honey – or was it just that he was trying to recapture a relationship that had already run its course? He'd been so excited when he and the psychiatrist had been reunited over a case the previous year, but he evidently hadn't been as content as he'd thought he was. He granted that she was very beautiful, but he'd previously seen beyond that beauty and sadly found a person he didn't think he could trust thoroughly.

Feeling rather miserable about this gradual realisation, he drove home and found the house empty. Not one of his pets was indoors. Going out into the back garden he called the cats fruitlessly for some time, then went inside to get himself a sandwich. When he'd eaten, he took another few minutes outside, calling to his missing Abyssinian, then gave up. The animal clearly wasn't anywhere close by. If she had been, she'd have come bounding back at his call. Monkey really was very intelligent and that was why, he thought, that he missed her presence so much.

When he got back to the office, he had determined to have a last look through Annie Symons' things, but was immediately distracted by the ringing of his telephone. It was Tomlinson again, to inform him that he'd gone to the employment agency and discovered that they had set up an interview for Melanie Saunders as a live-in member of staff with Jefferson Grammaticus at The Manse. The man hadn't mentioned that when they'd visited his establishment when the body had been discovered. But then, if she hadn't turned up for the interview, and the woman wasn't known to be missing, why would he – except for the fact that her body had been found in the grounds of his hotel. Had he actually known her and was covering up?

He'd have to go back, and he'd take Carmichael with him again. Grammaticus was a slippery customer, getting up to all sorts of tricks with his staff, as they had found out when they originally met him. Although he didn't think he'd resort to murder, it had to be checked out. While he waited for his sergeant's return, knowing that he would take his full lunch break as he was going back again to Castle Farthing to see how Kerry was feeling, he made that call to Ruth Lockwood.

The vicar's wife remembered him from his investigation in Shepford Stacey and greeted him cordially. 'Surely not *another* murder in our little community?' she asked.

'Not at all. I'm just making enquiries about a loose end we didn't tie up when my sergeant and I were there before. The woman who lived in Copse View who wasn't in residence at the time: have you got any firm news of where she had gone?'

'How funny you should ask that. The property's just been sold. Why do you ask?'

'Just checking up on her welfare,' he replied without a sliver of guilt in his conscience. 'I don't suppose you happen to remember the name of the estate agents?'

'It was a Market Darley agency. Leavitt and Quitte, I believe, but I'm afraid I don't know who was responsible for its sale.'

'That's OK. I can pop in there myself and get any information I need. Thanks for your help, Mrs Lockwood.'

'Anytime, Inspector. Nice to hear from you. You will let me know, won't you, about anything you find out? I'm a real nosy parker.'

'Mrs Lockwood, you are a mine of interesting and useful information.'

'How kind of you. Good day.'

He ended the call as Carmichael breezed back in to his desk. 'That was the vicar's wife from Shepford Stacey,' he informed the sergeant. 'Fanny Anstruther's house has just been sold,' he explained, then added, as an afterthought, 'How is Kerry?' He was really hopeless at other people's personal lives, as well as his own.

'To be honest, sir, she's feeling pretty awful. I'm quite worried about her.'

'Well, I'm sorry to hear that, but we've got to go down to The Manse again. You've got your mobile, haven't you, so that she can contact you in an emergency? And you can take your own car in case something does arise. It's a lot closer to Castle Farthing from The Manse than it is via Market Darley to pick up your car. And afterwards, I'd like you to accompany me to an estate agents in town called Leavitt and Quitte.'

Carmichael's face had dropped at the word 'emergency', but he nodded, and Falconer explained about Tomlinson's latest round of information. 'We need to know when the interview was – although Tomlinson could find that out if he dug hard enough – we have to know whether she turned up for it, and we're going to have to be on the look-out for signs of lying. If she did arrive, did she leave again?'

'I can believe a lot of things of Grammaticus, but I don't really see him as a killer, sir.'

'I'm with you on that one, but we have to be sure, and we need to establish a date for her disappearance, even if it's only a date when she didn't turn up for something. Come on, Sergeant, let's get this over with so that you can be on hand if anything develops with Kerry. Perhaps she's just coming down with a cold or 'flu.'

'I hope that's all, sir.' Carmichael's face was lugubrious as he about-turned and prepared to leave the office once more.

Chapter Eight

The Manse really was a bit swish, and it looked imposing as they turned through the enormous – and no doubt very expensive – metal gates. It had the look of a stately home about it, but a friendly one, and wasn't in the very imposing Gothic revival style which was common in the local area: it was softer and considerably more welcoming. The gravel drive wound through immaculately manicured lawns and well-kept flower beds to the large studded oak double doors that led to the interior.

This time they had the element of surprise, and Jefferson Grammaticus was astounded to see them back in his hotel so soon. 'What is it now, gentlemen? Has another body been traced to my premises?' he said, arising from behind his huge desk and holding out a chubby hand to greet them as they entered his office unannounced.

'Not at all, sir,' Falconer reassured him. 'It's just that the remains we recovered before have turned out not to be those of the person we were looking for, but are of a totally different young woman. Look, I'm not explaining this very well, so I'll just cut to the chase. We have reason to believe that you had an appointment to interview this young woman for a live-in post when you were setting up your hotel, and we'd like to know if she kept the appointment and was deemed unsuitable.'

'Give me her name and I'll check with my records. Mind you, that'll only tell us if she was interviewed. I suppose you want to know whether she turned up or not.' Damn, the man was quick.

'She was referred by an employment agency in Market Darley, if that helps to jog your memory,' added Falconer, still not letting go of her name.

'There was someone. I'll just check with my diary. There was so much going on at the time that I can't recall the details.'

Opening a desk drawer and pulling out an A4-sized 2010 diary the hotelier leafed through it to when he was hiring staff, just prior to the opening of the establishment, and pointed excitedly at an entry not long before they had received their first guests.

'Melanie Saunders,' he stated. 'Didn't turn up for the interview. There it is in black and white. Is that who you're after?'

Falconer gazed over and glanced at the entry. This, in itself, didn't prove anything, and the man could have prepared for this eventuality in advance if he was responsible for the remains found on the edge of his drive, but Falconer didn't think so. If he had been, why would he have allowed the workmen to uncover what was left of her, and then phone the station in such a temper? No one was that devious – were they?

'The agency was hopeless, as I recall, and only had one client on its books who was willing to undertake domestic work. I wasn't at all surprised when she didn't turn up for her interview.'

'So you never met her? She wasn't one of your ex-cons?'

'Never, and no she wasn't! And if she wasn't reliable enough to turn up for an interview, she wouldn't have been reliable enough to employ.' Grammaticus' world was very monochrome: there were no shades of grey with him.

'She may not have even been alive by the time of the interview,' Falconer suggested.

'God, I hadn't thought of that.' The man was appalled at the thought. 'And you think she may have been out there since then?' In his distressed response, he ran his stubby fingers through his tightly curling hair, their progress halting suddenly as they re-encountered a recently acquired bald patch. A fleeting moment of surprise washed across his face at this rediscovery.

'There doesn't seem to be any other explanation. She told her neighbours she was going for the live-in job, and when they didn't see her again, they thought she'd got it and moved in.'

'How ghastly! Obviously, neither I nor my staff had any idea.'

Falconer sighed heavily before he voiced his next request. 'I would like you to provide the names of all the contractors who would have had access to this site immediately before she was due for interview.'

'It'll be a pretty long list. We were nearing opening, and there were all sorts of snagging jobs and last-minute work going on.'

'And a list of your employees at the time.' Falconer thought that the body had not been interred by someone who would go on working there, but he had to be sure – especially since Grammaticus, with his experience of the legal profession, had employed a cabal of former criminals of his acquaintance. It seemed to him highly likely, that someone, who had or was working there at the time, had taken advantage of the disturbed earth that creating the drive had entailed, and used this to mask the hiding of the body.

'I'm going to have to email that lot to you. I can't just produce it at the drop of a hat. And it'll be a long list. I presume you want Ms Ironmonger's name left off?'

'Not at all. One never knows,' replied Falconer with a little frisson of horror that it could have been Meep's previous owner who was responsible for this body, as well as the other souls she'd previously polished off.

'You're right, of course. One should never make assumptions. Do you want to speak to anyone else while you're here?'

'I think we'll leave that until after we have all the names, but thank you for the offer, Mr Grammaticus.'

Falconer sighed. This could have been done with a phone call, but he'd been so upset by being carpeted in the superintendent's office that he had wanted to be seen to be doing his job.

As they exited the building Carmichael's mobile rang, and he answered it to find a near-hysterical Kerry on the other end. His body seemed to snap to attention, all the colour drained from his face, and his bottom lip began to quiver. He ended the brief conversation before turning to the inspector and saying, in sepulchral tones, 'That was Kerry. She seems to have gone into labour weeks early. I have to go. Now!' He hared off immediately to his battered old Skoda as if all the hounds of hell were after him. That didn't sound good. Falconer may not have been any good at dates, but he knew Kerry's due date wasn't this month.

Falconer dropped in at the station to pick up Tomlinson for his visit to the estate agents, and made the mistake of asking the DC about himself. The man had been a fairly quiet soul until now, but he had obviously reached the stage where he felt he could open up to his new superior officer – and boy did he open up!

Carmichael drove back to Castle Farthing with his right foot on the floor of his car. Fortunately, being an old Skoda, it didn't travel at very high speeds and, although his driving was erratic, he wasn't really in any danger.

He threw himself out of the driving seat and barged into Jasmine Cottage in a total panic, and found Kerry in a similar condition. Now, during

111

his time in plain clothes, he had learnt to control his outward expression of feelings, with the exception of the reaction of his stomach to certain stimuli, and found that he was able to exude a false aura of calm. After calling an ambulance, having ascertained that the signs of labour had not abated, he sat his wife down and made her a cup of tea, speaking to her soothingly.

Kerry was terrified that she was going to lose their babies. Carmichael spent this intervening period persuading her that she wasn't: that everything would be fine, and that they would survive, even if they had to be born this early. He must have been very convincing, because Kerry soon perked up and began to look on the bright side.

Her husband collected the birth bag she had already packed for her stay in hospital, and loaded this into the ambulance with her when it arrived, promising that he would follow behind in the car. He couldn't go in it with her, because he'd have no means of getting home, as regular public transport wasn't a thing that existed in village life. He also needed to drop Harriet at his mother's house, and arrange for his parents to collect the boys from school.

It was a cumbersome arrangement that meant that he would have to have his mother staying in the village if Kerry was admitted and kept in. Not giving a fig for how complicated life was going to get, he merely drove, his daughter strapped into the baby seat in the back, and finally gave way to his feelings.

As he made his way to the town, he had tears of distress pouring down his cheeks, and his body heaved with gigantic sobs. How could fate be so cruel as to threaten their expected children's lives?

'Why didn't you just drop her at the shop with Rosemary and then give us a ring?' his mother asked, as he dropped off his young daughter, and suddenly he felt a complete fool. That would have been the sensible and logical thing to do, and through all his feigned calm he had not even thought of this.

He left his childhood home with a promise from Mr and Mrs Carmichael senior that they would head straight back to Jasmine Cottage, and that he should leave everything to them. It was just a pity that his mother didn't drive, or she could have managed on her own. With a mental 'duh', Carmichael got back in the driving seat of his jalopy and set off for the hospital.

When he arrived, he found Kerry on a labour ward with a cannula in her arm, and a clear fluid dripping down into it. 'What the hell's going on?' was his immediate reaction, with a quick glance to check that she still had her huge bump.

'It's OK,' she reassured him. 'It's to stop the labour and keep them in there a bit longer, and the pains are lessening, so I think we'll all be all right.'

'How do you feel?'

'A lot calmer, and not in so much pain. Davey, whatever will we do if we lose them?' She had experienced a quick volte-face in mood.

'Come on, I thought you sounded upbeat. Where's that famous "always look on the bright side of life" outlook that you usually have?'

'I think it got drowned in fear.'

'That's no attitude for a mother who's carrying

twins. You don't want them born depressed, do you?'

'I don't want them born at all at the moment.'

'It'll all be fine,' he said, but without much conviction. Maybe it wouldn't. Such things happened to other people – why not to them? Why would God consider them special? He didn't really believe in such a supreme being but, in times of extreme stress, reverted to a faith he once had possessed as a child.

The two of them stared into each other's eyes and both burst into tears attracting a nurse to come over and reassure them that everything that could be done was being done and, for a while, they believed her.

'We'll have to keep Mrs C in to monitor what's happening, so if you have any arrangements to make, I suggest that you do that now,' she said, in a calm, soothing voice.

'The kids are already sorted out, but I have to phone my boss and let him know that I won't be back, at least for today,' he replied.

'You get off and do it then. Your wife will be just fine here.' The nurse said this with such confidence that Carmichael, feeling suddenly more positive, went outside to use his mobile phone.

'...and I seem to have settled in quite well here, but I do miss the dramatic scenery of Cornwall. I mean, it's all very pretty round here, but where are the craggy hills, the walled narrow lanes? And I miss the old, abandoned tin mines and the wildness of the sea. And my mother. And my brother. And the accent's so bland up here. At least in Cornwall it's got a bit of character,' Tomlinson rambled in his West Country voice.

'I don't know if I could settle long-term up here. Eventually, I'd like to go back down west and take Imi with me. It's a great place to raise children – loads of open countryside for them to ramble in, and the beaches are fabulous. Then, when they're older, there's surfing and sailing, and climbing. All that exploring. Grand place it is, and I miss it sorely.'

This had been going on for the last ten minutes, and the DC seemed to be having a fair ramble of his own, as they approached their destination. 'Here we are,' declared Falconer, not adding, '...at last. Now, shut up'. He admired enthusiasm and honesty from his officers, but this was a bit much.

'Sorry about going on a bit, but Imi's free time hasn't coincided with my hours much, and I miss having someone to talk to.' Suddenly, the inspector missed Carmichael. The sergeant would have appreciated someone with such a love of their native soil, as he was a natural advocate for 'round here', and would have given Tomlinson a good run for his money, as well as not finding the subject boring. And where was Monkey? The little cat intruded into his thoughts once again as the car pulled up outside the estate agents.

Mr Quitte, one of the original partners, was on holiday at the moment, but Mr Leavitt Jnr was available if they'd just wait a minute. Mr Leavitt Jnr proved to be a man well on in years but still with an enthusiastic twinkle in his eye. He beckoned the two officers to the other side of his desk in an office off the main area and asked them how

115

he could help them, as they held out their warrant cards. 'Moving in together are we?' he asked. 'Moving out of the station house?'

'Absolutely not,' spluttered Falconer. 'We're making official enquiries about a property you have recently sold.'

'So sorry if I've offended you,' retorted the elderly man, 'but so many gay gentlemen are investing in joint properties now. I think it may be to introduce a stabilising effect on their relationship.'

'We're just colleagues,' added the inspector, just to get things straight, only to be answered with,

'Oh, very coy. I won't be shocked, you know. I'm very broad-minded.'

'Well, I'm not.' Falconer was getting rather flustered at the estate agent's insistence. 'Now, can we give you the address that we're enquiring about and get this thing started?'

'Oh, dear! I try so hard to be understanding, and now I've upset you.'

'Copse View in Shepford Stacey,' Falconer almost yelled in his frustration.

'Copse View, eh?' Mr Leavitt cogitated for a moment. 'Now, that's rather difficult.'

'How? We only want to know who was responsible for putting it on the market.'

'It's still rather difficult.'

'Well, did you sell it or not?'

'Yes, but the work was carried out by our Mr Quitte.'

'And your problem is?'

'Mr Quitte was originally my father's partner and has not yet got to grips with computers, given his age. He conducts all the sales that he super-

116

vises on paper and through telephonic communications, and he writes everything down in a paper file.'

'Can we have the file, then, so that we can ascertain who the vendor was?'

'Well, that, in itself, is the problem. He took that particular file home with him, as it was due to complete just the day before he went away on holiday, and he hasn't brought it back yet. It did complete on time, and he let us know to put up a sold board but, as yet, I don't have any details of who sold the property, or who bought it.'

'Has anyone come in to collect keys?'

'Not as yet, I'm afraid.'

'So, you've sold a property. You don't know the name of the vendor or the purchaser, you've erected a board, and all without you having any knowledge of such important data?'

'That would seem to be the case. It's never been a problem in the past.' Mr Leavitt looked a little crestfallen.

'Do you have a contact number at Mr Quitte's holiday address?'

Mr Leavitt actually blushed as he replied, 'I'm afraid we don't. We just bumble along, and we've never had any problems before.'

'When will he be back?'

'Not for another fortnight. He always takes a long winter holiday because he says he can't stand the weather here.'

'Absolutely bloody marvellous – I apologise for my language, sir. I didn't mean to say that aloud. Please get in touch with us when he returns,' spluttered Falconer, passing over a business card.

As they left the building, he could just hear a low mumbling from Tomlinson. 'Bloody batty old fart. How he and Quitte haven't run the business into the bloody ground is un-bloody-believable.'

'Did you say something, Constable?'

'No, sir.'

'Good. I don't approve of bad language.'

Chapter Nine

Falconer's mobile rang and, on answering it, he found Carmichael on the other end. 'I wonder if you could do me a favour, sir?' he asked meekly.

'Carmichael, whatever's going on? Is everything all right? How's Kerry?'

'They've put her on a drip to stop the contractions, and she's fine, but I'm going to stay over in Market Darley and I don't have anything with me. I need a bag of stuff.'

'Where are you going to stay?'

'In one of the relatives' rooms at the hospital.'

'But what about the children?' asked Falconer, hoping, as soon as the words were out of his mouth, that Carmichael wasn't going to ask if they could stay at his house.

'That's what I was about to explain. My mother's in Castle Farthing taking care of that side of things and I've already phoned her to ask her to throw some things into a bag for me, so I wondered if you'd mind collecting it and bringing it over to the hospital. My mum doesn't drive

118

and I don't want my father driving more than is necessary, but I don't want to leave Kerry on her own at this stage. She's very fragile in her state of mind.' He didn't add what a similar position of fragility he was in, too. He could cover his agitation and worry for a short while. 'Please, sir.'

'No problem, Carmichael. And you stay with her as long as you need to; I've still got Tomlinson to work alongside me – although I shall miss your unique company.' That was a bit below the belt, but he was worried too, on his sergeant's behalf, and a little unmindful of what he was saying. 'I'll get the bag to you as soon as I can.'

'Thank you, sir.'

Tomlinson had had some responses to the notes he had left through the letterboxes of the houses in Drovers Lane; he could spend some time working out who needed talking to in person, and whom he could deal with on the telephone. He was perfectly capable of making appointments for himself, and could take himself off there to carry out the interviews without the inspector holding his hand. So distracted was he by Carmichael's situation, that he never called to mind the fact that he and the sergeant always worked together.

It wasn't long before Falconer found himself outside Jasmine Cottage and knocking at the door. There was a deep baying from the other side, which aroused his forgotten fears about Mulligan, followed by a high-pitched whining, and Mrs Carmichael senior opened up. 'Ah, the great detective arrives,' she announced, in tones that he could not positively identify as sarcastic. 'Come on in and I'll get Davey's bag for you.'

Falconer stepped gingerly into the main room and, to his surprise, saw Mulligan lying on the floor by the kitchen doorway, his face a mask of longing as he gazed at his beloved. 'Whatever have you done to that dog?' he asked, perplexed. He'd never seen the huge hound so subdued before.

'I've given him a good telling off about his behaviour and, so far, he's being a good boy, aren't you, Mulligan dear?' She pronounced the second half of this sentence with her head turned over her shoulder, a wolfish smile slapped across her face. Mulligan panted with fear, and gazed with apology at the object of his affections, as if to say, I'd love to come over and give you a good licking, but this lady has told me off about being over-demonstrative.

'Hello, Mulligan,' he ventured tentatively, and the dog hung his head, as if he were ashamed of his subdued behaviour.

'Mulligan's a good dog now, aren't you, boy?' she announced, as she headed for the stairs to collect her son's overnight things. 'And you stay where you are.' Falconer didn't know whether this was directed to the dog or to himself, so he just stood where he was and waited.

When she returned with a holdall, she stared at him, by the door and asked, 'Why didn't you sit down?' So, it was to the dog she had been speaking.

'Oh, I spend too much of my working life in a chair. Just stretching my legs, sort of,' he replied, lamely, taking the handles of the bag from her. She only came up to his chin but she was like Russian vodka; a short went a long way. 'Well, I'll

120

be off now. I don't want to disturb you any longer than I have to.'

Accepting the pathetic excuse for why he had not moved a step, she said 'Give my love to Davey and Kerry, will you?' and dismissed him from her mind, allowing him to see himself out and shut the door behind him. As it closed he heard another whine from the Great Dane, as if in apology. Falconer was with Mulligan on this one: the woman terrified him, but then she must have had to be quite strict with so many children to bring up. He could have done with a lot more like her when he was in the army. They would have terrified the enemy.

When he returned to the office, still completely stunned by the dog's reaction to Carmichael's mother, he found it empty, and a note from Tomlinson telling him he had now heard back from all the residents of Drovers Lane, and had considered it more time-efficient to actually go over and speak to them in person. Ha! thought the inspector, a way of getting more cups of tea and coffee, more like, and then sloping off for a prolonged lunch without returning to the office.

Taking this as a sign that he could do the same himself, he put on his answerphone and rushed off home to have another check for whether or not his pet had returned home. Chivers would have a fit if he knew that the three CID officers were AWOL, but Falconer simply didn't care. He would watch the public appeal that night on television and then appear as if he was up to speed.

Tomlinson had made arrangements to visit the

residents of Drovers Lane in one fell swoop, receiving assurances that those who had not been there on his previous visit spoke to him either on their lunch break or in an extended version of it.

He started at number eight, his summons at the door answered by a bald-headed man who introduced himself as Mr Brixton. He was a farm labourer and lived alone. On being asked, he said that he had only lived in the cottage for six months, since his job had commenced, and had no knowledge previously of Annie Symons – in fact, had never heard the name before. He was a non-drinker who had never frequented the local pub and was, therefore, not conversant with village gossip. The DC believed him and moved on to number seven.

Number seven revealed a Mr Cassidy who was semi-retired, and admitted to being able to recognise the previous occupant of number two, but claimed that he had never spoken to her. He was divorced and lived alone. No luck so far.

Mike Mortimer, as the resident of number six introduced himself, claimed to be a general builder and odd-job man. He also declared that he had not known Ms Symons – but there was something about the way he avoided eye contact that Tomlinson didn't take to, and he decided that this character could do with some checking out.

He asked if the man had a card he could take, noted that he had a website, and determined to check him out as soon as he got back to the office. If there were any recommendations on it, he could contact some of his previous clients to get their opinions on the trustworthiness of this Mortimer.

Number three housed a man of similar employment. Simeon Perkins stated that sometimes he and Mortimer worked together on jobs, but this was not often, as most of his work consisted of fairly small jobs, and he only infrequently got involved in bigger works that needed more than one man. Of Annie Symons, he declared virtually no knowledge. 'I used to say good day to her, that's all, if we were out in the back or front gardens at the same time,' the man stated.

There was something about this man also that disturbed the DC, but he had a sneaking suspicion that it was probably because so many of his friends back in Cornwall had been duped out of more money than they had been expecting to spend by one of this ilk. He also claimed to be contactable via the internet, and Tomlinson thought that here was another one he could check out from his previous clients. How strange, he thought, that little one-man-bands like this were computer-contactable, when the established estate agents he had visited earlier lacked this necessary modern facility to business.

Perkins, after claiming to have been barely on nodding terms with Annie Symons, ended the conversation quite abruptly, saying he had to get to an appointment with a client.

In his enthusiasm for his impending internet-searching task, Tomlinson got back to the office rather earlier than he intended, and was therefore present when a call came in to let the police know that a cache of handbags had been uncovered on some scrubland by a metal detectorist.

Meanwhile, Harry Falconer had trailed disconsolately round his house and garden again, feeling rather subdued and convinced that his pet was dead or stolen. There could be no other reason for her to disappear. After a rather unappetising sandwich of ham that needed using up, he got to his feet, ready to go back to the office and the case in which he, at the moment, had little interest.

In the Market Darley hospital, Carmichael sat by his wife's bed, following a scan that had revealed that the twins were well-developed and of a good size.

'Are you certain that your contractions have stopped, love?'

'There's absolutely nothing now, Davey. Don't be such a worry-guts. They said they'll keep me in for a few days, and then I should be able to go back home, as long as I rest.'

'I'll get my mother to stay on. You can't go running around after three kids and rest.'

'Much as it goes against the grain, I'll agree.' Kerry visibly winced. 'Oh my God!'

'What's wrong? Is it the pains starting again?' Carmichael's voice and face were filled with concern, as her hand began to tremble in his.

'I'm not incontinent yet, Davey, so that means that my waters must have broken. Quick! Get a nurse. This is serious.'

Carmichael fumbled with the call button until he managed to summon somebody to their aid. 'You know what this means, don't you?' said Kerry in a husky voice. She drew back the covers and revealed the wet patch on the bottom sheet as he looked on with horror.

'No! Tell me.'

'It means that I'll have to deliver them. It's like the seal's gone on a jar, and they're susceptible to infection. It's going to have to go ahead, and we'll just have to hope that they're both OK.'

For the second time that day, Carmichael felt a deep depression and panic rush over him, despite the doctors' reassurances that the twins were likely to be fine. Sometimes he felt that he and Kerry had been too lucky thus far in their marriage. Everything, in retrospect, looked too easy.

In fact, he had never been so overwhelmed with such a swirling mass of conflicting emotions. He was excited and elated to think he was finally going to meet his children, worried about Kerry and how she would fare with a double birth, and terrified and preparing for grief in case something went wrong. He was full of such strong feelings that he felt his heart would surely burst. Without any effort on his part, his eyes began to leak again.

As Falconer sloped back to the office DC Tomlinson came rushing out, a look of eagerness on his face. 'A metal detectorist has uncovered a stash of handbags on some waste ground. Now, it may have nothing to do with our case, but it's evidence of some crime or another. Proper job! People don't just bury handbags for the fun of it, me old lover,' he crowed.

Falconer perked up at this and was in full agreement, deciding to forgive this Cornish endearment – this time. It was probably just because the lad was excited about a possible development, but he shouldn't try it again or Falconer would have to

have words with him. He wasn't *anyone's* old lover
– yet! As they rushed down the stairs, though,
Tomlinson seemed to be blissfully unaware of the
casual manner in which he had referred to his
senior officer.

'Where were they found? When were they
found? How many of them are there?' Falconer
was back in the game, glad at this distraction from
his unhappiness. 'They could have been taken as
trophies, and now our murderer knows we're on
to him – or her, but that's rather unlikely – he's
got rid of them.'

The stash was waiting for them about a mile
outside Coldwater Pryors, guarded by the metal
detectorist who had found them and who introduced himself as Jonas Preston. He explained that
he was a student who passed his free time looking
for 'buried treasure'; quite apt as he was studying
archaeology. It had taken Falconer some fancy
footwork to get over the rough ground from the
road, made more difficult by trampled lengths of
barbed wire fencing and large tussocks of un-
yielding couch grass, and he had had to fight to
keep his balance.

After introductions had been made and warrant
cards displayed, Falconer asked, 'How deep were
they buried? How did you come to find them?'

'They weren't very deep,' replied the student
with the red hair and beard. 'Only about a foot
down, but I noticed the earth had been disturbed. I wouldn't normally come out here, as I
live in Nether Darley, but I have a colleague
online who said he'd found some Roman coins
down here. It was sheer luck that I chose this bit

of ground. And that's when I saw a disturbance to the grasses and the earth.

'One of the reasons I decided to dig here was because I thought maybe someone had already found something here, but might not have dug deep enough, and sure enough, I got a bleeping straight away, so I knew there was metal down there. I just didn't expect it to be handbag buckles and zips.'

Falconer pulled out his mobile phone and then broke all the rules. He put on some gloves and lifted one of the handbags out of the hole. He then photographed it, and did the same with the rest of the cache. Then he put them back where he had found them.

'Now we've got something to work with, I'll summon some CSIs.'

'Sir, should you really have done that?'

'No, Tomlinson, I should not. But then, I didn't, did I?'

'Of course not.'

'Hey, you're a cool dude,' commented Jonas Preston, seemingly impressed with this maverick attitude to rules and regulations.

'Well, you carry on checking out the ground round here while we wait for someone with another car to come and take you back to the station, and we'll go and look at these photos in my car.'

'Chilly, Boss,' replied Jonas, who had never had any positive dealings with the police before and was finding them more human than he expected from what his fellow students had told him.

Sheltered from the biting wind, Falconer held his camera out and went through the photographs one by one, sharing the small screen with Tomlinson. 'What do you think, Constable?'

After a few moments silence while Tomlinson got his thoughts together, he announced, 'I think they were trophies, but that the finding of two of the bodies has panicked the murderer, and he doesn't want to be found with these bags in his possession.'

'That's very good reasoning, Tomlinson. Now, why would we find them?'

'Because it's someone who thinks we're going to call round?'

'OK, let's go through any suspects we have. We might as well do this out here, instead of just wasting time waiting around.'

'We could do with checking out the landlord who's supposedly in France. I only have a French mobile number for him, so he could actually be in the UK.'

'Good thinking, lad.' Tomlinson, apart from his eulogies on Cornwall, was proving to be a steady and thoughtful officer. 'And I rather fancy the other landlord, our Mr Colin Bridger. He was a bit too good to be true.'

'And there are those two guys who are builders in Drovers Lane, one the neighbour of Ms Symons. They were both very shifty, to my mind.'

'That's a fairly good start. We can question those four again, but in the station this time. So, what have we got as far as these trophy bags go? No expensive makes. A red fake crocodile skin, a pink plastic model, by the looks of it. This brown one I considered to be of fairly good-quality leather. And there was a denim one and a green suede one.

We'll have to wait to see if any fingerprints turn up on them, and I bet they've been emptied of all their contents. Life couldn't be *that* generous to us.'

'We'll just have to rely on the fact that he was probably in a panic when he disposed of them, and was a bit careless.' Not only was Tomlinson efficient, but he was also optimistic. This partner- ship could work well in the absence of Car- michael. DC Roberts' replacement was certainly an improvement on the original model.

Staggering over, once more, to Jonas Preston, they explained that they would now leave him to the tender care of the soon-to-arrive CSIs until a uniformed officer arrived, who would not only take him to the station to make his statement, but bring him back to this site. They then began to make their way back to the car.

'I can see the CSI car coming down the road. I'll just go and hand over to them, and then we can get back to the station, while you phone in and arrange for our man to be picked up,' said Falconer, pointing at a vehicle approaching from the direction of Market Darley.

As Falconer and Tomlinson continued to head towards the road to pass on their witness, the DC suddenly found he was walking on his own, con- temporaneously with the sound of a voice exclaiming, 'Bum!'

Turning round, he discovered the DI flat out, face down, and wearing a fair covering of cow dung. He had slipped on an elderly cow pat which had not washed away in the recent rains, and was now retching into the grass at the smell.

Damn it, thought Falconer, as soon as I don't have Carmichael, I begin acting like him. He suddenly really missed his DS for a second or two. Carmichael may seem sloppy but, in actual fact, the DI knew, he was anything but.

Fortunately, one of the CSIs removed a newspaper from the boot of the car and passed it silently to the now noxious detective, and intoned, 'I always carry a couple in case of accidents that I don't want to transfer to the car's upholstery.'

'Thank you. I wouldn't want to soil the inside of my car.' Falconer took the proffered periodical meekly. 'Perhaps I ought to nip off home when I've dropped you at the station, and get cleaned up and changed.'

'Very good, sir.' Tomlinson could barely speak for trying to smother his laughter.

Chapter Ten

When DC Tomlinson got home that night, Imi was, as usual, baking like a demon. She didn't seem to be able to stop since he had moved in – probably some sort of subconscious desire to feed her man – and had so far, managed a dozen fairy cakes, which she was icing when he came through the door, sixteen scones, a fruit cake, and three quiches.

Smiling with delight, he said, in a mock-serious voice, 'How on earth are we going to be able to cope with all this?'

'You never put on an ounce. You'll cope,' she replied, turning round to smile at him. 'Come here and give me a kiss.'

That sorted, she poured him a beer and led him to the sofa. 'You just sit down and catch your breath. I'm sure you've had a busy day.'

'Found a cache of evidence today, although I can't tell you about it.'

Imogen smiled. She was the soul of discretion, and she knew he would, when he was sufficiently relaxed, so she just got on with her icing and waited. 'What sort of a day have you had?' he asked.

'A bakey sort of one; which is just as well, as I enjoy baking so much. Oh, by the way, I thought I'd do a steak and kidney stew overnight and do us a pie or a pudding tomorrow. Which would you prefer?'

'Pudding,' he replied with food lust in his voice. 'What shift are you on tomorrow?' he asked, savouring his drink.

'One that most people would consider normal.'

'That being?'

'Eight till four,' she supplied, somewhat slurred as she was licking her fingers at the time. Baking she loved; messy was her method.

'Well, at least you've had a better day than Davey Carmichael's wife. She's gone into labour with twins, and is in the hospital in absolute agony. Davey's gone to be with her.'

'How's he going to eat tonight if he's on duty holding her hand and mopping her brow?'

'Hadn't thought about it. Why?'

'Just give me half an hour,' she replied, rinsing

out her large mixing bowl.

Falconer dribbled out of the office a bit later than his constable, and made his way home moodily, preparing himself mentally for watching Chivers lording it all over ordinary policemen on television. He'd have to tune in, but he'd hate every moment of it. Sometimes he thought the superintendent left a trail of slime behind him when he was dealing with the media.

On his way he had picked up a Vietnamese takeaway to try to cheer himself up, and he even set the food in china serving dishes so that it looked like he had made it himself. Using a large serving spoon, he filled a plate and sat down to begin eating. As he did so, he got up and switched on the television so that he could watch the news on the local programme and was just shoving a chopstick full of noodles into his mouth when Chivers' smug face appeared.

It was actually on the national news, and he nearly choked on his food at the shock of this. That meant that now they would be hounded by the media. Great! As the familiar voice droned on, the face trying to look sincere and concerned, the inspector heard the cat flap clock a few times, but did not count how many cats had come in. That was an easy one, as they would all assemble round his chair begging for scraps; they weren't fussy and were quite international in their tastes. Yes, there were the four regular suspects.

Above their begging meows, however, he heard a faint chirrup and looked behind him to see a very bedraggled Monkey sitting just inside the kitchen door. She was dirty and thin but the sight of her lifted his spirits so much that he leapt from his chair and rushed over to pick her up and embrace her, covering her begrimed face with kisses of joy.

He had no idea where she'd been, but she definitely smelled of mice and, boy, was she filthy. He hugged her to his face, repeating her name and dancing round the room with her in his delight, and the only solution that he could reach was that she had been locked in somewhere while someone was away for a few days; maybe a garage or something. He didn't care. She was back, and that's all that mattered.

Putting her down carefully on the work surface, he got some food out of the fridge for her, then set it down and put her beside it and the water bowl. Poor, starved little creature. She, eager to relate her misadventure, 'talked' all the time she was chewing and swallowing, and she definitely sounded cross with herself that she had not been home for so long.

'Oh frabjous day, calloo, callay,' sang her owner, and continued to sing the rest of the poem to a tune he had never heard before, while he watched her scoffing and moaning. The other cats hadn't gathered round her, however, and he went back to the table to find them on top of it, consuming his meal with guilty enthusiasm, not only from his plate, but from the serving dishes as well. And he didn't care, so happy was he. He'd get some toast if he was hungry.

Amidst all this outpouring of joy, the doorbell rang, and he went quizzically to answer this surprise summons, for he was expecting no visitors.

Tomlinson arrived at the hospital, entering the maternity ward with a feeling of gross embarrassment. He had not expected to find himself in a place like this for some time to come. Moans, groans, and actual screams occasionally issued from doors when nurses opened them to get in and out. In his hand he had a carrier bag with enough food in it to feed an army, a contribution to the sergeant's welfare that Imi had thought worth making.

A very officious nurse – or midwife, for he didn't know the difference – bustled up to him and bristled as she asked him what he was doing there, for she hadn't recognised him as one of her 'fathers'.

'I've just brought some food for Davey Carmichael,' he said, hoping that he wasn't about to get a detention. 'I believe that his wife is in here in labour.'

'I'll fetch Father for you. I don't believe that Mother's at a crucial stage at the moment; but for a minute only. His wife needs him,' she snapped back at him with a flash of her gimlet eyes, making him feel very like a naughty schoolboy caught, infected, by the nit-nurse.

Carmichael was ushered out of a door through which very profane language was issuing, and the sergeant blushed at the sound. 'She's in transition,' he explained, 'and apparently that can let out some very ripe words.' His face was as red as a tomato as even worse language followed it. 'It's normal ... or so I'm told.'

'Has your wife ever been in the navy?' the DC

134

quipped, only deepening his colleague's embarrassment.

'You just wait until it's your turn,' retorted Carmichael, although he had missed the birth of his daughter Harriet, as she had been delivered by Harry Falconer, in circumstances on which we shall not dwell.

'Daaaveyyy!' Kerry roared out from the labour room. Carmichael grabbed the carrier bag gratefully, and was already nosing inside at its contents before he got back inside the room. By God, he was starving.

'Thank you for your time,' whispered Tomlinson to the nurse who had fetched the sergeant.

'Thank you for your consideration and thought,' she replied, and unexpectedly smiled at him, proving that she was human, and not one of the devil's minions.

When Falconer opened the door with the widest grin he could manage without inflicting actual damage to his facial muscles, he found Honey on the doorstep looking up at him nervously.

She had considered this visit long and hard. She had been unfaithful to him when she was in the Caribbean and had subsequently undergone an abortion – something that Falconer, with his formal and old-fashioned outlook on life, had found very hard to deal with – but she bitterly regretted her foolish actions of the past, and had really missed him when he had called her for all the harlots under the sun and dumped her.

Eventually, she had begun to think that she really had not valued him for what he was: a good-looking, upright, very moral and admirable man who did an extremely difficult job very well. He was definitely husband material, especially when compared to her cheap fling on the island, and she had been an utter and complete fool to play around with his feelings the way she had.

She had been very grateful when she had bumped into him on a case last year, and he had tentatively asked her out again. She had felt that things were going quite well, although they did not see each other as often as she'd liked, and then to be dumped like that, as if she were just a distraction to his job, was unbelievable. Honey Dubois was only just getting to the point where she realised just how much the relationship meant to her, and she was going to get it back on track whatever that took.

At least he seemed to be in a good mood, she thought, as he flung wide the door and greeted her, his face grinning as widely as that of the Cheshire Cat.

'My Monkey's come back!' he announced, making it sound as though it were a totally understandable statement.

'What?' She didn't even know he had a monkey.

'My little Abyssinian cat,' he explained, picking up same and waltzing around with her, with a paw in one hand. 'This is Monkey, and she's been missing for days. This calls for champagne! Will you join me?' he asked with a chortle of glee.

'I've never been known to refuse champagne,' Honey replied, thinking that it was as if he'd never given her her marching orders.

He put down the little cat and disappeared into

the kitchen. She heard the fridge door, then the hiss as the cork surrendered, and he walked back in with a bottle and two flutes. 'Be my guest, and the toast will be "To my little Monkey".'

Honey perched on the edge of the sofa and took a glass, now overflowing with bubbles. 'To your little monkey,' she said, forgetting to give the name a capital letter in her haste. Falconer perched beside her, his glass raised, took a sip, and then looked deep into her eyes. Not a thought of Serena marred his thoughts.

'Harry,' she said.

'Shhh. Don't say a word. Let's just drink to a very happy occasion,' he replied, and drained his glass. She did the same, and he refilled them. 'Down the hatch! There's more where this bottle came from.'

Honey didn't look a gift horse in the mouth, and did as she was told, the way a proper lady should. She was truly a reformed woman – and one on a mission, now.

Chapter Eleven

In the local maternity ward, Kerry Carmichael was grasping her husband's hand so hard that he was panting along with her. Apart from a spasm of pain, his main facial expression was one of determination. Their daughter Harriet had been born at home, but although the sergeant had physically been in attendance, he was, unfortunately, unconscious, having passed out with the shock of what he was witnessing.

Thank God DI Falconer had been there to come to her assistance, although the senior detective and Kerry had been a bit embarrassed round each other for the next few meetings, after he had experienced such an intimate view of her anatomy. This time her husband just had to be there for her. He had to be!

'You're doing very well, Mrs Carmichael,' pronounced the doctor, who had insisted on being present as it was a double birth.

'Carry on the way you're going, Mum, and it'll all soon be over,' the midwife encouraged her.

'More pain relief. I can't stand it anymore,' groaned Kerry.

'Just give a really big push. The first head is crowning,' said the midwife in attendance. 'That's it, and one more should see it out.'

'Aaaaargh!' screamed Kerry.

'Ooof!' moaned Carmichael, his eyes as big as saucers as he lost consciousness, his head coming into sharp contact with the metal frame of the delivery bed, the rest of his body folding up like a concertina.

'Come along there, Mr Carmichael. Come on round, that's the way to do it.'

Carmichael opened his eyes to discover that he was lying flat on a casualty bed in A&E and that there was a dressing on his forehead.

'I'm afraid you had a little mishap, sir,' explained one of the nurses gently.

'Where's my wife? What did she have? What's

going on?' Carmichael felt completely dis-orientated, as his hand floated up to his forehead and felt a dressing there.

'You had a little knock to the head, but you'll be fine after a bit of a lie down. We don't think there will be any concussion. Just a few stitches, that's all.'

'But I was in a delivery suite on maternity,' he babbled, sitting up.

'That is correct, sir. Now, if you'll just lie still...'

'Where's my wife. What am I the father of?'

'A baby, I expect.'

'No, you don't understand. She was having twins, and early twins at that. There should be two babies.'

'Have we been wetting baby's head a little early, perhaps?'

'Let me up off here. I want to see my wife and my babies. Oh, please God that they're all right.'

'I really think you should calm yourself,' said the nurse, putting her hand flat against his chest, when the midwife from the delivery suite came along the line and stopped by his trolley.

'Ah, Mr Carmichael, I've been looking for you. Your wife would like to see you now.'

'How long have I been here?'

'You've been on that trolley slumbering like a baby for about two hours,' replied the nurse.

'Oh, my God. My babies! How are they? What are they?'

'Plural?' asked the nurse, in puzzlement.

'Mr Carmichael here has just become the father of beautiful twins.' The midwife looked smug.

'But what sex are they?' Carmichael shouted

in frustration.

'Why, you have one of each, sir: a beautiful girl and a bouncing boy – both lustily healthy, although a bit small.'

Carmichael fainted again and rolled off the trolley.

Harry Falconer floated gently up from sleep without the usual clangour of his clock to wake him, and couldn't understand why he was feeling so happy. Hang on a minute. He wasn't in this bed on his own ... there was someone with him. Why would there be someone else in his bed? Who would have the audacity to break in and get into bed beside him? Surely, he must be dreaming.

And then he remembered and, almost simultaneously, Honey's naked body snuggled up beside him.

How could he? They weren't married. They'd broken up. How could he behave in such an ungentlemanly manner?

A light butterfly of a kiss landed on his exposed shoulder, and he turned his head. Honey looked like a cat that had got the cream; a woman who had achieved her mission. And then he saw the time. Christ Almighty! It was *nine o'clock*, and he was still in bed. Usually he had been in the office for over an hour by now.

'Harry?' a seductive voice enquired from the next pillow, and then something happened for which he had been totally unprepared, as a dainty little hand sneaked towards him under the covers.

Chapter Twelve

'Good morning, just, sir,' Tomlinson greeted him. 'This isn't like you at all, nearly eleven o'clock.'

'Oh, didn't I mention that I had a dental check-up this morning?' lied the inspector, hiding his blush by turning towards his desk.

'I must've missed that, sir. By the way, I took a bag of food into the sergeant yesterday evening. Just to keep him going. It was Imi's idea.'

God! Carmichael! He hadn't spared him a thought since the evening before. 'And how was he?'

'Having to put up with his wife swearing like an old-time sailor.'

'That doesn't sound like Kerry.'

'Apparently it's something to do with the labour process. I didn't ask. There are only so many things in this world that a man wants to know about.'

'Quite right, Constable.' Falconer didn't want to go there either. He'd made one trip before, and didn't like it, when he'd delivered Harriet. Disconnecting from the conversation, he sat at his desk, his mind awhirl. One evening, and his life had changed so much, and he was only just getting back the memories, which had been formed, encased in champagne bubbles. How had that happened? And he was changed forever! This may not have been a big deal for any other man, but for

Falconer, it was a truly life-changing situation.

Silence reigned in the office as both men applied themselves to their paperwork, but the inspector was finding it hard to concentrate, with the visions that kept arriving, unbidden, in his mind.

Finally, Tomlinson spoke again. 'Did you see the TV appeal last night?'

'Er, yes, I did catch it. Maybe it'll stir people's memories,' Falconer replied, still with his head down to hide his confusion.

As if this were a prophecy, Tomlinson took two telephone calls in quick succession. With a gleam in his eye, he turned to the inspector and said, 'Well, that appeal worked a treat. It's got all the old gossips out.'

'Have you been playing Grass Thy Neighbour with the lace curtain brigade?'

'What? Oh, I see what you mean. Yes, I suppose I have. That was an old biddy from Castle Farthing who says that your landlord of the property in Drovers Lane, Mr Bridger, was seen regularly in the village visiting Annie Symons. Another informed me that the chap who supposedly lived in France who owns the property in Stoney Cross was only there for a year, and has been back for some time.'

'But he had a French mobile number,' countered Falconer.

'Apparently he finds it rather useful to retain that French phone for anonymity purposes, as I suggested yesterday, when we went out to speak to that metal detectorist. Those two facts will certainly give us something to chew on.'

'Let's get to it, Constable. Have we got a note

of the addresses?'

'Oh yes indeed we have, sir. Got 'em right here.'

'Who were the phone calls from?'

'The first one was an acquaintance of Bridger's wife from WI, so she knew him by sight and knew he owned the cottage, and the second was from the next-door neighbour of our supposed Francophile.'

Colin Bridger was a different animal on home territory. When faced with the fact that there had been a statement to the effect that he used to visit Annie Symons, he became blustering and confrontational, but this was probably because his wife was at home and present at the interview.

Eventually, Falconer said that they would be better continuing the conversation down at the station, and they led him away, much to Bridger's unexpressed relief.

In an interview room, he came clean, but said he couldn't have admitted this silly dalliance in front of his wife, and that it wasn't sexual, but that he and Annie Symons had been writing a children's book together, something he had always wanted to do. He might have held his hands up at home if it had been an affair, but writing a story about pixies and elves was too silly for words, and he couldn't have admitted this to his wife – she would have laughed at him.

'And how many times, in all, did you visit her alone in her home?' asked the inspector.

'I don't know. I didn't make a note in my diary in case my wife found it and thought what you just did.'

'There doesn't seem to be any evidence of your input on the manuscript which, in fact, we have taken possession of.'

'I wasn't going to be credited. It was just for fun.'

'So, why didn't you say anything when she disappeared?'

'I thought that she had done a runner, so I re-let the property. We'd just about finished the story, and I thought she'd just get on with trying to get it published on her own. In the end, I didn't think it was any good anyway. It was only a daft dream of mine that I've had since I was a child. I just wanted to get it out of my system.'

'We shall want to take your fingerprints, sir,' stated Falconer, his mind on the handbags.

'So that you can eliminate them from your enquiries?'

'Something like that.' Falconer didn't think so, but he wouldn't say anything at the moment. Let the man think his story about fairies had gone down well. But, he didn't believe it for a moment. For now, he had another line dangling in the water, and he wanted to see if he could land his fish. He'd make his mind up later.

They found Timothy Driscoll, the so-called French resident, at home and very surprised to see them. 'We contacted you by telephone before,' explained Falconer after introductions had been made, 'and I don't remember you mentioning that you were resident in the UK again.'

'Ah, yes. Sorry about that. I don't like to advertise the fact that I've come back.'

'Got a lot of debts, have you?' asked Tomlinson.

'Not really. I just don't want people knowing I

failed to make a mark on the French way of life. I was so enthusiastic before I went that I rather dug myself a hole and, when it didn't work out how I had hoped that it would, I didn't want everyone knowing I'd had to slink back here with my tail between my legs.'

'You mean it didn't work out financially?'

'It didn't work out, full stop. I couldn't get the hang of the language, so I couldn't work, and if I couldn't work, then I couldn't live. I don't make enough from those flats to keep me.'

'I understood you didn't charge very high rents,' put in Falconer.

'Yes, that's true, but it only made it even more impossible for me to do them up, and nothing's selling these days, is it? I couldn't put the rents up as they are, I couldn't afford to renovate them, and I didn't stand an ice cube's chance in hell of selling them for more than tuppence ha'penny. You see my dilemma? Anyway, I hadn't received a penny of rent from that property in I don't know how long and I had no idea until I came back from France that she had gone, as she never answered any of my letters. I just knew that I wasn't being paid.'

'So why didn't you re-let the property?' queried Carmichael as Falconer wrinkled his nose in distaste at the thought of the state of the flat.

'Have you seen it?' asked Driscoll. 'I haven't got the sort of money that that place needs spending on it to make it lettable.'

Falconer wasn't feeling particularly sympathetic towards a man who had hoped he could either just pick another life in a foreign country, without putting any work in, or live off investments, and

145

gave him a very old-fashioned look. 'So you've come back here. And are you working?'

'No. I'm having to live off benefits. I can't find a job.'

'Shame!'

What a waste of time this had proved to be.

That afternoon brought news from Forensics. Of the handbags recovered from the site the day before, there had been no fingerprints. There were five bags in all, and one of them proved to have a concealed inner pocket in which they had found a store card belonging to Ms Suzie Doidge.

'So that's one of our missing girls. We've found the bodies of Melanie Saunders and Annie Symons, we've got the body of Suzie Doidge still missing, this Natalie Jones has supposedly disappeared and there's Fanny Anstruther, not to mention Wanda Warwick's friend Bonnie Fletcher. No wonder the national press got on to it. It's turning into rather a complex case, Tomlinson. Hang on! There wouldn't be any bag for Natalie Jones. She's just gone missing, so whose is the fifth bag?'

'Oh, we've had fair wonders of cases down in Cornwall, sir. You wouldn't believe the complexity of some of them.' And Falconer was thoroughly distracted. 'Now, I remember, when I was first in uniform...'

The inspector got to the point where he almost lost consciousness with the wonders of Cornwall, when a wave of what had happened the evening before washed over him, and suddenly he had to sit closer to his desk so as not to advertise the evi-

146

dence. He had now completely lost his train of thought.

The internal phone rang, bringing him back to normality, and he found Bob Bryant on the line. 'We've had a call from some builders down in Ford Hollow – you know, that place where you had all that trouble last year – and it would seem that they've uncovered a woman's body. I think you and Tomlinson ought to go and take a look. It sounds like it might be another one in the same pattern.'

'We're on our way, Bob. Whereabouts in Ford Hollow?'

Whereabouts in Ford Hollow turned out to be on the edge of the village, where the ford had been recently diverted to allow the building of new houses, much to the disapproval of many of the residents. One of the machines digging the foundations had uncovered the remains of a body, partly rotted but still recognisable as a young woman.

Rev. Florrie Feldman met them at the site, where she had been alerted he was arriving. 'You killing off your parishioners again?' Falconer hailed her as they approached the now dormant and sleeping digger.

'You cheeky whippersnapper! Let me explain. The digger was scraping the ground prior to starting to dig the foundations, when it uncovered an unexpected occupant under the surface. She's a bit raggedy, but I'm sure I'd recognise her if she were one of mine.'

'Not if she was already in there before you took over,' the inspector countered.

147

'True, true, but we've had quite a lot of the locals out here to have a look – you know how fast the grapevine works in a village – and none of them said anything about recognising her. Of course, they turned up on the pretext of having a last protest at the granting of permission to build here, but I could see it in their eyes that they were just rubbernecking. After all, the ford has already been diverted, so there was really nothing that could be done about the situation.'

'Nothing gets past you, does it, Rev.?'

This particular member of the cloth had come to Ford Hollow the previous year, just before there were a couple of very nasty incidents, but she had originally met Falconer when in her first parish of Shepford St Bernard, and they had forged the beginnings of an alliance. They got on well, and Falconer felt that he could always trust her word, which is why he had turned to her quite recently when he needed someone outside of the station to talk to.

A CSI team was at work, and Doc Christmas had already pronounced life extinct – beyond all hope. 'That's three dead and two missing,' announced Tomlinson unnecessarily, and not much help to Falconer to recover the thread he had picked up earlier and nearly run with, and had now totally lost.

'Did we get DNA samples taken from the house in King George III Terrace?'

'We did indeed, sir. Who do you think this is?'

'I think it's got to be our missing Ms Doidge, although I suppose it could be Bonnie Fletcher or Fanny Anstruther – but unlikely to be our

Miss Jones, as this body has a long-buried look to it. Do you know, I just can't seem to see the pattern to this. Why kill three or four young girls and an old lady, unless the old lady was a practice murder and set the pattern for all the rest. Our Fanny doesn't quite fit into this story.'

'When did Ms Doidge disappear, to our knowledge?'

'She hasn't been seen since April 2009,' replied Falconer after a quick wrack of his brains.

'What a rats' maze this case is.'

'You can say that again, Tomlinson.'

Back in Market Darley, the station was besieged by press, so news must have already leaked out about the discovery of yet another body, and they had to fight their way through the scrum of bodies, mumbling 'No comment' as they did so.

'I hope you two didn't give anything away,' called Bob Bryant, as they passed his desk. Was the man *ever* off duty?

'No. It was a real pleasure to tell them that we had no comment, instead of our interviews being littered with the dratted phrase,' Falconer slung over his shoulder, and it was. He could count on the fingers of one huge mob how many times that expression had been used against him in interview, and it was a real pleasure to get his own back.

'Oh, and a Mrs Littlemore phoned you. I've put the number on your desk.'

'Thanks, Bob.' Now, why did *she* want to talk to him?

Amy Littlemore and her husband Malcolm lived in Steynham St Michael, and were married

149

to the bottle rather than to each other. They ran a craft shop but were more often than not, drunk in charge of a commercial establishment.

He retrieved the number from records and rang, only to find a very proper and sober voice answering the phone. 'Is that Mrs Littlemore?' he asked, hardly able to believe that it wasn't a neighbour or friend.

'Speaking. Is that DI Falconer? I seem to recognise your voice.'

'It is. How perceptive of you.'

'Oh, I was waiting for your call. And, by the way, in case you're wondering, I've given up the drink. It would've killed me if I'd carried on the way I was going, and Malcolm's shown solidarity and given up too.'

'How's business?'

'Booming, now we're sober behind the counter. But it was about that TV appeal by your superintendent that I phoned originally. Such a handsome man, and so very compassionate, in my opinion.'

'Go on,' urged the inspector, grinding his teeth at these off-the-cuff compliments about his senior officer. He'd not pass those on. The man's head would get so big he'd need a good coating of lard just to get through his office door.

'We used to have an assistant who came in for a few hours a week, and suddenly she didn't come in anymore. Well, that was OK when I was, er, imbibing, but when I became sober I got to thinking about it. It was rather odd, her just not turning up like that, and I thought I'd better speak to you about it.'

Surely not *another* one? 'What was her name?'

'Marilyn Slade. Mousy little thing. I doubt we've seen her in a couple of years now. This was just an enquiry to see if she was all right, really.'

'Where did she live?'

'Prince Albert Terrace, here in Steynham St Michael, but of course she could've moved. I tried calling her number, but it's no longer in existence, and I had a quick peek through the window of her place but she doesn't seem to be there anymore. I didn't dare be any more nosy in case the neighbours thought I was up to something. That was this morning, you understand. I couldn't have done that when I was, um, tired and emotional all the time. Can I leave it with you?'

'We'll check it out, Mrs Littlemore. Thanks for your concern, and congratulations on giving up the demon drink.'

'It wasn't easy, but we both managed it, and life is much better now. Thank you for calling me back, Inspector.'

'What was that all about?' asked Tomlinson.

'A woman from one of my early cases with Carmichael. She used to be a terrible drunk, but she's reformed now, and she's just noticed that someone may have disappeared. What is this all about? There won't be a woman left in the county if we carry on like this.'

'Don't exaggerate, sir.'

'I'm not. Look how many there are so far, and I knew nothing about any of them – but it isn't just me who doesn't notice. It would seem that no one else takes much notice of who's around them anymore.'

'It's modern life, sir. It goes at such a pace that people don't take much notice if someone stops showing up.'

'But these are the "villages", Tomlinson, and they always used to.'

'Evidently not, sir, if what you say is true.'

'Bum! You're right. But I just can't see the pattern to this case. It seems to be all young women, and there's Fanny Anstruther, a pensioner, right at the beginning of it all.'

'She's had them, sir,' crowed a familiar voice on the phone.

'Congratulations, Carmichael. What did she have?'

'A boy and a girl. I'm so excited. I've got to go home this evening, but can I delay my paternity leave as previously asked, because my mother's coping?'

'Of course you can.'

'Only, Kerry's got to stay in with the twins because they're a bit small, and my mother said she could stay until Kerry comes home.'

'That's fine. Tomlinson's covering for you admirably.'

There was a short silence of disapproval after this remark, then, 'Could you meet me for a drink tonight in The Fisherman's Flies to wet the babies' heads? Only I won't be going back to the hospital, and I'd like to get out for an hour or so.'

'Is there not a friend or family member you'd rather go with?' Falconer was flattered but thought he was an odd choice of companion.

'No, sir. I think of *you*, out of working hours, as

my friend.' The sergeant was on cloud nine, and forgot to be reticent about his feelings.

'Well, thank you very much, Carmichael. The feeling is reciprocated.' Falconer was still on cloud nine, too, after the evening before and the same thing applied. 'What time shall I get there?'

'Seven-ish?'

'Fine. I'll be there.'

Carmichael concluded the call on his mobile just outside the hospital, his head now swathed in bandages from his two falls, but he was a deeply happy man, and a few stitches didn't matter now that he knew Kerry and the twins were all right.

When Falconer arrived in The Fisherman's Flies that evening, Carmichael's ramshackle figure was already propping up the bar. He wasn't yet drunk, but the sheer happiness of what had happened had left him grinning from ear to ear.

'What'll you have, sir? I'm having a pint to celebrate.'

'Just a half for me. You can stagger home, but I need to drive.'

'My mum wouldn't mind if you stayed over. You could always bunk in with me,' the sergeant offered.

Considering the terrifying thought of seeing Mrs Carmichael senior and sharing a bed with his sergeant, not to mention the more than likely possibility that Mulligan would sneak upstairs and join them meant that Falconer refused as politely as he could. He said that Honey might pop round tonight – if he was very, very lucky – and his little Abyssinian hadn't been home long,

153

and would miss him if he weren't there.

Carmichael was too elated to take offence, and immediately ordered himself another pint. As they raised their glasses to the new lives, George Covington stopped by them and said, 'I knew all those girls that were on that there appeal the other night. We always record the national news for after we've closed, so that we can keep up to date with events for the punters.'

'What, all of them?' asked Falconer, in disbelief.

'All of them. All the young 'uns come out here, you know. Right magnet this is for young people. Don't know why.'

'Did you know a Marilyn Slade as well?'

George thought for a moment, then said, 'I believe I do, as it happens, although I can't say as I've seen 'er in a long while.'

'Who's that, sir?' This was a new name on Carmichael, although he'd kept fairly up to date by phoning Bob Bryant all through Kerry's labour, until he'd passed out.

'Come over to this table here and I'll tell you.' The inspector led Carmichael away from the bar and passed on the latest snippet of information from Steynham St Michael.

'So, whose was the latest body found?' the sergeant asked.

'Don't know whether it was Suzie Doidge or Marilyn Slade. It was too long deceased to be Natalie Jones, that's for sure. And all these women have been disappearing while we've been working together and we knew nothing about it. They're like an invisible string of beads drawn throughout our time together, and it's only coming to the surface now.'

'Wow! Unbelievable!' Carmichael was suitably impressed, if not suitably sombre. 'I'm going to come in tomorrow afternoon, after I've visited the hospital and made the arrangements with Mum. I want to be in on this one. But, for now I need another drink, and I'll probably have a sore head in the morning.'

'I'll finish this one and leave you to it.' Falconer had other fish to fry.

On arriving at his own house, he found Honey on the doorstep. How could one man be so lucky?

The cats had ignored Honey that morning, turning their backs on her censoriously when she had floated down the stairs, but they did hear something that they approved of during the hours of darkness that night. 'Don't do that. It's disgusting!' floated down to their ears, and they were reassured that their owner still had some standards left.

Chapter Thirteen

The next morning, Falconer arrived at the station on time, but still floating around in the stratosphere in his mind, but Tomlinson soon brought him back to earth with a bump. 'We've had some identification on that body that was found at Ford Hollow, sir. It was Marilyn Slade. She's on our records because she was once arrested for shoplifting.'

'Not Suzie Doidge?'

'No, sir.'

'Well, where the devil *is* that woman?'

'Don't know, sir.'

'Neither do I, Constable, and that's what's perplexing me. Have you requested a CSI team to go round to this new victim's address?'

'Yes, sir.'

'But, I had a very interesting conversation with the landlord of The Fisherman's Flies in Castle Farthing last night, which I think we ought to take into consideration.'

Tomlinson was as staggered as Falconer had been about George knowing the girls but Falconer still wasn't happy about the Anstruther woman, a situation which handily resolved itself when Reverend Lockwood phoned at that point.

'Sorry to bother you, Inspector, but Ruth told me about your enquires regarding old Fanny, and I thought I ought to let you know that a nursing home has just contacted me to say that she has died in their care, but that she had asked to be buried within our parish. Nobody told me that she'd been admitted into a home, so I couldn't advise you of her whereabouts any sooner. I'm just arranging the funeral now.

'Apparently a distant relative arranged the sale of the house so that her fees could be paid, as her cash had run out, but this is the first I've known of the situation.'

That sorted out Falconer's gut feeling that the old lady's disappearance didn't figure in the series of murders, but it didn't really leave him any further forwards with regard to the other women. 'Thank you very much for the information, Reverend. It was very public-spirited of you to let me know.'

'My duty, Inspector, my duty.'

'So, that's the old lady out of the picture, Tomlinson. Fanny Anstruther is dead, but in no suspicious circumstances. What are your feelings about the other deaths?'

'I'm still not happy about Perkins and Mortimer from Drovers Lane. There's just something about them. I don't know whether there's a guilty look in their eyes because they over-charge their customers, or whether I've just got a thing about their profession, but I think there's something not right there.'

'And I'd like a word with George Covington,' said Falconer, 'and the landlords of the Drovers Lane and the King George III Terrace properties aren't out of my suspicions yet.'

'What do you think we should do?'

'Get them all brought in for further questioning. And we need to visit the house in Prince Albert Terrace where Marilyn Slade lived. Let's get that out of the way first so that we can get a breath of fresh air.'

The press officer had been siphoning off all the reporters who had crowded the steps and taking them into the conference room to give them twice-daily updates, if there was anything, on Chivers' orders, so that they could exit the building without having to run the gauntlet of a mob of press, and for this they were grateful.

The superintendent was also bringing in a posse

of officers from other forces to conduct a search party for Natalie Jones. A lot of them would stay to cover the legwork on the current murder investigations, as it was obviously too much for a small station like Market Darley to cover. For this Falconer was grateful, as all the information gathered and sifted would be passed straight to him as SIO. Chivers had already stated that he wanted to hang on to these investigations, and it was obvious that he wanted all the glory when they were solved.

Tomlinson and Falconer drove straight to Steynham St Michael and called in to Knitty Gritty to see if Amy Littlemore had any more information. She had remembered nothing else, which was hardly surprising, considering the state in which she usually struggled through life, but Malcolm had come up with a rather fuzzy photograph he had taken of Amy and Marilyn, when she first worked for them.

'She was here a couple of years,' he informed the detectives.

'And you never enquired after her when she just didn't turn up for work?'

'You know how things were then, Inspector. We didn't know what day it was, let alone how long she'd been gone, when we were on the sauce.'

'It was only that TV appeal that jogged our memories. We'd almost forgotten that she used to work for us then your superintendent made us remember her, and realise that she might actually have disappeared,' explained Amy. Falconer knew when to be grateful for small mercies. Marilyn Slade evidently wasn't a victim over-burdened with family or friends, just like the others, and it was a chilling thought, how many women such as these could go missing without anyone being any the wiser, except for a passing thought here or there.

The house in Prince Albert Terrace was a tiny Victorian build. Nothing about it was particularly smart or modern with the exception of the front door, which was visibly newer than the window frames and the interior fittings. It was grubby and neglected both inside and out, with the exception of this door. The kitchen fittings were sixties-style, the bathroom, ditto, and the wiring looked like it hadn't been updated for a long time either.

As with the other houses of victims, there were clothes in the wardrobe and chest of drawers, toiletries in the bathroom, and make-up on the dressing table: another Marie Celeste mystery for them to solve.

There was also a CSI team flinging grey finger-print powder around with gay abandon, and Falconer, who had momentarily forgotten that he had unleashed this team, blustered at them that they'd need to sort through everything for evidence that might help them with the case. Of course the CSIs already knew this and were actively engaged in doing just that, but he felt he had to save face somehow at blundering in on them in the middle of their search.

'Did you mention we were getting Carmichael back this afternoon?' asked Tomlinson, apropos of nothing, as they slunk from the house, slightly red-faced at this unexpected meeting of officers.

'We are indeed, and we'll need to get him up

to speed.'

'I understand, from office gossip, that the super's doing another appeal tonight.'

'Typical, but it won't do any harm. Best get back, and get those suspects brought in. Actually, scratch Driscoll. We still don't have a body, but we can bring in both Covingtons. You and I can do the interviews, while Carmichael updates himself.'

DS Carmichael was waiting for them when they returned to the station. 'How are things?' asked the inspector.

'The twins are doing well, and Kerry's more rested now. I'll pop in on my way home this evening. She knows the score with this job, so she won't be too upset that I don't spend hours by her bed. We haven't thought of any names yet, so she can occupy her mind with that.' Carmichael raised a hand to Tomlinson and added, 'By the way, thanks for the scoff you brought in. My stomach thought my throat was cut.'

'No problem, mate.'

'Good good good.' Falconer recaptured the lead. 'Now, let us tell you what you missed.'

Bridger brought in his solicitor, having phoned him when the car arrived, and picked him up on the way. The interview went as expected.

'Falconer: You are Colin Bridger, the owner of 2 Drovers Lane, Castle Farthing?

Bridger: Yes.

Falconer: You had a relationship with your tenant, Ms Annie Symons?

Bridger: No comment.

160

Falconer: Was your relationship in any way sexual?

Bridger: No comment.

Falconer: Did you have anything to do with the disappearance of Ms Symons?

Bridger: No comment.

Falconer: Did you do any harm to Ms Symons?

Bridger: No comment.

Falconer: Were you responsible for the death of Ms Symons?

Bridger: No comment.

Falconer: Did you conceal her body in Castle Farthing woods?

Bridger: We've already discussed why I knew Annie. No comment.

Falconer (in exasperation): Would you like cod and chips this evening?

Bridger: Yes, please.

Falconer: Then buy it yourself. Interview terminated...'

Or, at least this was how Falconer related the interview to Carmichael afterwards, with a surprisingly good imitation of Bridger's voice. He was feeling unusually upbeat today, even given his lack of grip on the case.

George and Paula Covington were another case entirely. For one thing, there was no solicitor present, and for another, they were more than willing to have a chat with Falconer and Tomlinson.

'**Falconer**: Mr Covington, you stated to me last night that you knew the women about whom our superintendent put out a television appeal: that would be Annie Symons, Melanie Saunders,

Fanny Anstruther, Suzie Doidge, and Natalie Jones, the first two dead, the other three missing? And did you also know Bonnie Fletcher or Marilyn Slade?' This last one he had added as the most recently identified body.

George: I know all of them, except the third one you mentioned, but we've both met the others. Two of them worked for us, but you already knew that. And are the last two missing or dead as well?

Falconer: The first, missing, the second, unfortunately, also dead.

Paula: Whatever is the world coming to? But to clarify, we've met just about everyone who lives in Castle Farthing, and Market Darley, and a good number of the villages.

George: The Fisherman's Flies is a popular pub.

Paula: Everyone comes out to us, especially in the summer.

Falconer: Did you know them outside of work?

Paula: Well, I used to bump into Annie sometimes in Allsorts – you know, the little shop?

George: No.

They both spoke their answers together.

Falconer: Do either of you have any idea how they could have disappeared or been murdered?

Paula: How dare you!

George: No.

Falconer: I mean, did you perhaps ever overhear anything in the bar that might have made you suspicious?

Paula: I just let the chatter go in one ear and out the other.

George: No.

Paula: We had a barmaid disappear on us once

162

in London, didn't we George? Never did find out what happened to her. Probably ran off with her fancy fella, if truth be told.

George: Don't remember that, Paula love.

Paula: Course you do.

George: No I don't.

Paula: That there flighty one who was always flirting with the customers. And you didn't help matters when she flirted with you and you flirted right back at her.

George: Did I?

Paula: Yes, you did. A woman notices these things.

George: Can't say as I can place her; there have been so many barmaids over the years.

Paula: George, you're hopeless, you are, with your memory.'

'I didn't know you were so good sir, at impersonations, but that sounded just right,' said Carmichael, both taken aback and impressed with his senior officer's levity. This was unheard of.

The rest of the interview had been similarly unhelpful, but Falconer's interest had been spiked by the mention of a woman who had disappeared from their previous establishment, and he made a mental note to get in touch with the brewery, and perhaps interview them again separately. Was George just playing the old duffer? Did he really have a sinister past? Was he that good an actor? And surely he was past it. Many a murderer had put on a good front, though, while concealing heinous deeds. And should he bring Peregrine and Tarquin in as well? Good God! He couldn't think straight because of Honey.

Unfortunately, the brewery that owned The Fisherman's Flies was very unhelpful about casual staff and could not give them any information even if they'd had it. This was due to something that was referred to as 'human rights', data protection, or some such nonsense, though Falconer could see little about human rights for the victims in this case. In the middle of the afternoon, however, the diligent hum of the office was disturbed by the trilling of the outside line, and Falconer answered it to find a furious Sadie Palister on the line.

She was a sculptress whom he and Carmichael had met on the case they had investigated in Stoney Cross, when they had originally met Reverend Ravenscastle and Peregrine and Tarquin. At the moment she was spitting fire, insisting that he come out to the Mill, which Falconer remembered was her friend and fellow artist Araminta Wingfield-Heyes' house. She was more or less hysterical, but all he could get out of her was, 'There's something in the lavatory that you need to see. And you need to come here right away and do something about it. It's an utter disgrace.'

Apart from that, he could get no sense out of her, but knowing what a pragmatic, if somewhat unpredictable, person she was at times, he decided that he really ought to take a look. There had been something about her tone that not only brooked no argument, but that had the seeds of something really disturbing about it.

'Come along, Carmichael,' he said, out of long habit more than anything else. 'Hold the fort, Tomlinson. We're off to Stoney Cross again.' Tom-

164

linson grimaced, feeling he had been shrugged off like an out-of-favour concubine.

'What was the phone call about?' asked Carmichael as they went down the stairs.

'It was Sadie Palister saying that there was something horrible down her lavatory,' the inspector explained bluntly, 'or rather, down Araminta Wingfield-Heyes'.'

'I know how she feels, sir. There's often something horrible down mine as well, but that's usually one of the boys not flushing when they've finished.'

'I have a feeling she meant something even more sinister than that, Sergeant.'

When they arrived at the Mill, the sculptress answered the door and bade them enter, where they found Araminta Wingfield-Heyes sobbing on the sofa. The former still wore unashamedly gothic make-up and sported her long waterfall of jet black hair, her nails painted to match. The latter was a little bit chubbier than she had been at their last meeting, but her cropped mousy hair had grown considerably.

'It's absolutely ghastly, Inspector,' declared Araminta – Minty to her friends – now considerably calmer than just a moment ago. 'Take him to see it, Sadie. We don't know what to do about it.'

'Come with me, you two, and make it snappy,' barked Palister in her usual brusque manner. 'I've had to use a bucket since we phoned you. I was too desperate to nip home.' The hysterics on the phone had been a surprise, as nothing usually upset this strong woman, and what was all this about a bucket? She led them to a bathroom on the ground floor, walked towards the lavatory, screwed up her face in disgust, and pointed down the pan as she stood there, pointedly looking in the other direction. 'Just look down there,' she ordered them, and the two men walked tentatively over to stare down the pan.

'Whoa!' yelped the sergeant in surprise.

'Well, well, well,' mused the inspector in a more measured fashion.

What was staring up at him from the bottom of the pan was a skeletal hand, its index finger pointing upwards. 'It was me that found it as I went to squat over it,' stated Sadie, 'And I had such a shock that I damned near cacked myself. Minty had total hysterics when I showed her. Where the hell has it come from, and what does it mean?' she asked. 'And when are you going to arrange for it to be taken away?'

'I don't know, as yet, Miss Palister, but I shall get a team over to investigate as soon as I can. Is this property on mains drainage?'

'No. The village has only got septic tanks.'

'That should make life easier, then, for the men searching.'

'So, what will Minty do in the meantime?'

'Can she stay with you? I remember your studio from when I was here before.'

'She can, but how long will this take? I mean, you've got to take that thing out, haven't you?'

'I can't say with any accuracy how long that will be, but I'll do my best to hurry it along, as it compromises the drainage system at Miss Wingfield-Heyes' home. It's lucky she's got a friend like

166

you who can put her up.'

'It is, isn't it, Inspector,' agreed Miss Palister with sarcasm, and she stomped out of the bathroom calling, 'Come on, Minty. You're going to have a little stay at mine, so you ought to pack a bag. Get your nose wiped and get a move on. We don't want to delay these intrepid officers any longer than necessary,' she concluded in a very slightly shaky voice. She had been uncharacteristically unsettled by this outrageous discovery.

The four of them left the Mill together, Minty locking up behind them. 'There'll be a key at my studio when you get someone to come over and get that disgusting thing out of Minty's loo,' Sadie said.

As they walked towards the car, Falconer exclaimed, 'Bloody hell! Part of another body. What the hell has been going on? Somebody's been on an out-and-out killing spree and we've known absolutely nothing about it.'

'Could this be one of our missing girls?' asked the sergeant. 'Obviously not Natalie Jones, because she's only just gone missing.'

Falconer stopped and stood for a moment, in thought. 'Could be. We just have to hope it is either Bonnie Fletcher or Suzie Doidge, but I get the feeling we're never going to find the latter. We'll have to have a good team meeting when we get back to establish exactly where we are. There seem to have been so many stray bodies come to light, and so many missing people, that my head's in quite a whirl. In the meantime, Carmichael, get Uniform to seal the scene and we will send the CSI team tomorrow.'

They arrived back to a sulking Tomlinson. He'd become used to being the one who was working with Falconer, and he had not appreciated just being dumped – but there were two builders who had been brought in for questioning, and any bad feelings would have to wait for later, as would their case summary.

Mortimer was furious at being dragged away from his work at such short notice, and was angry with himself for telling a colleague where he was working that day. He had thought he could trust Simeon Perkins not to let him get dragged away from earning a crust, but Perkins had been taken in for questioning too. It was just both their misfortunes that Perkins had been collecting some tools from home when the police car turned up, and he'd thought, if he had to go in, why shouldn't Mortimer?

They exchanged glances as they were led almost simultaneously to interview rooms, and Falconer and Tomlinson went in to Mortimer first. It seemed only fair that the DC should do these interviews with him, as he had been the one to deal with residents from Drovers Lane in the initial stages of the case, this action a small consolation for being left behind when the other two had gone over to Stoney Cross.

'Can you confirm for the tape your name and address?' asked the inspector, after recording the officers present and the date.

'Michael Mortimer of six, Drovers Lane, Castle Farthing,' he answered, with a glare.

'We are making enquiries about the death of

Annie Symons, resident at number two. I know you've already been spoken to, but I need to ask you a number of additional questions,' stated Falconer. 'How well did you know the deceased?' he continued.

'I only knew her to nod to,' he replied, not giving any additional information.

'Did you ever enter her house for any reason?'

'No.'

'Did you ever meet her socially?'

'No.'

'Did you see her in the local pub on any occasion?'

'Probably. The old biddy in the shop says she was a part-time barmaid there, but I've no memories of actually seeing her working there. So that had better be a no, then, as I can't place her behind the bar.'

Falconer sighed. As usual, they were getting nowhere fast. 'Did you ever bump into Ms Symons in the local shop?'

'Nope.'

After intense questioning for another fifteen minutes, it seemed that Mr Mortimer had seen Annie Symons leaving her house once or twice, but that had been the extent of his acquaintance with her.

'You said you didn't know her when I called round,' cut in Tomlinson, with some ire.

'That's because I didn't. I hardly think seeing her outside her front door and nodding to her was *knowing* her in any way,' Mortimer snapped back. 'That doesn't exactly count as bosom buddies, does it?'

Falconer could not carry on without some grounds, and decided to let Mr Mortimer go for the time being, moving to the next interview with his DC to talk to Mr Perkins.

The usual preliminaries taken care of with the tape, Falconer began, 'We're following up the previous enquiries made by DC Tomlinson here when he called on you at home, Mr Perkins. Do you have anything to add to that?'

'Absolutely nothing. I told your monkey here that I just said good day to my neighbour if I saw her in the garden, but I didn't know her beyond that. And I must say I object to being brought in here to be questioned on tape for something I know absolutely nothing about.' Perkins was visibly riled.

'You're not under caution, Mr Perkins. Although we're taping the interview, it's only for our records. Now, did you ever go into number two, Ms Symons' home, for any reason?'

'Absolutely not. Why should I be in the house of someone I barely know from Adam?'

'Did you ever do any work for Ms Symons?'

'She was only renting,' he replied with a grin of having got one over on them.

'Did you ever see Ms Symons when she was working in The Fisherman's Flies?' asked the inspector.

'Now, this is getting ridiculous. No comment,' replied the man, exasperating both officers.

'Did you ever go out with her?'

'I didn't know her.'

'Did you ever bump into her in the local shop?'

'No.'

And this was the tenor of the rest of the interview, leaving both the inspector and the DC absolutely exasperated. 'Well that did us a lot of good, didn't it,' stated Tomlinson, grinding his teeth in frustration.

'Right, let's sum this all up.' Falconer addressed his newly expanded murder team in the station's meeting room, which was the only space, apart from the conference room, big enough to hold them all. Apart from the three usual detectives, there were half a dozen DCs recruited from other forces to help with the volume of investigation of such an expanding case. 'It started with Carmichael, or rather his dogs, finding the body of Annie Symons in Castle Farthing woods.'

'Then there was Melanie Saunders, whose body was uncovered at The Manse,' added Tomlinson, almost defrosted.

'Not forgetting our most recently identified corpse, Marilyn Slade, who was uncovered in Ford Hollow,' the inspector chipped in.

'And we had Fanny Anstruther missing,' interjected Carmichael.

'Who turned out to be a red herring in all of this,' continued Falconer happily.

'And we've had Suzie Doidge missing all along.' It was Carmichael's turn again.

'And Bonnie Fletcher from Shepford St Bernard,' added Falconer.

'We've also got Natalie Jones, who's only just gone missing,' finished Tomlinson again, with a grin, his spirits fully recovered, having been

171

allowed to help with the interviews, unproductive though they were. 'I think we've got it.'

'It's a bit grim, isn't it, sir?' commented Carmichael.

'Absolutely frightful, and now we may have a body at the Mill in Stoney Cross,' agreed Falconer. 'The search party for Natalie Jones is underway, and we will put a team over at the Mill tomorrow to find out if there's anything else in the septic tank. We'd better attend as well, Carmichael.'

'But–' Carmichael started, with unease and a roiling stomach.

'But me, no buts, Sergeant. We're going, and that's it.'

Tomlinson grinned.

'But ... we're not exactly burdened with stunning suspects, are we?' Concluded the inspector with a rueful face. So many deaths and disappearances, and there were no obvious murderers. Then again, there'd been no obvious victims before these poor women's bodies started coming to light, and some of them had been missing quite a long time. He just hoped it wasn't going to be one of those unsolved mysteries with which police life is plagued.

'We've got Colin Bridger, the owner of number two Drovers Lane.' Tomlinson began to sum up the suspect situation, feeling he had more skin in the case than Carmichael, due to the latter's recent absence. 'If we find Suzie Doidge, we've got Timothy Driscoll. We've got those two iffy builders Perkins and Mortimer that we just interviewed, and we've got Old Man George Covington.'

'Not exactly rich pickings then, are they, Constable,' said the inspector wryly. 'Carmichael, I want you to organise our new DCs to undertake background searches on all of our suspects, with particular reference to the pub that the Covingtons used to run in London and the girl Mrs Covington said had disappeared.'

There was a moment's silence as the original trio contemplated their lack of progress. All they seemed to be good at was collecting corpses. Then the silence was broken by an undeterred Carmichael speaking in a stage whisper. 'Will you come with me to visit Kerry and the babies on the way home, sir? You can come as well, if you like, Tomlinson.'

'I'll leave it be, Sarge. I don't really know her. Yet.'

'I'd be delighted to, Carmichael.' Falconer had no formal arrangement with Honey for that evening, and he was still in a ridiculously cheery mood after what had been happening in his life over the last forty-eight hours.

Falconer dismissed his team to address the various tasks they had been allotted.

Chapter Fourteen

Kerry was waiting for them in a chair by her bed and took them to the nursery, where the twins were being kept under observation for a lot of the time. 'They should be let out and put by my bed soon,' she informed them. 'They each have to get to just over two kilos and then we can all go home. I don't really want to leave without them. Can I take them to the ward for a little while?' she asked the nursery nurse on duty, who nodded her head in approval.

Falconer took one crib and Carmichael the other, and they walked slowly back to Kerry's appointed place on the maternity ward. 'They're being absolute darlings,' she told them. 'I can have them by me for a few hours a day, and they hardly ever cry. I hope they're going to be as good as Harriet was.'

'Have you thought of any names yet?' asked her husband.

'Persephone and Apollo,' replied Kerry with an absolutely straight face, leaving Carmichael looking astounded at these outrageous suggestions.

'You can't mean that?' the sergeant exploded with outrage.

'I'm just taking a leaf out of your mother's book,' she said with a smile, then added, 'but the names are growing on me. And would you care to tell us both what your siblings are called?' Her eyes twinkled at this leading question.

Carmichael took the bait like a starving fish. 'Well, there's Romeo,' he began. 'Then there's Hamlet and Mercutio. We've got the girls next, Juliet and Imogen – same as Tomlinson's girlfriend, I never thought about that before – and, of course, baby Harry.'

'And what's your middle name, Davey?'

'Orsino,' he replied very slowly, suddenly realising how he had been reeled in.

'And can you think of anything better than my suggestions?'

Carmichael looked blank before suggesting, 'John and Mary?'

'You'd better be wearing black then, my dearest!' retorted Kerry with due gravity.

'Why's that?'

'Because it'll be over my dead body.'

'I see. Then I'd better leave it to you. I can get used to anything if you ask me to.'

'They're definitely growing on me,' said Kerry musingly before Falconer broke in by clearing his throat, and then they all took turns in holding the babies for a while. Carmichael was rock-steady, and cooed at them like the natural that he was. Falconer was a bit more pussy-footed, and held them as if they were made of fine porcelain, and he was liable to drop them. He considered that he would have been more comfortable holding a live shell.

After a reasonable amount of time they rose to go, and on the way out, Carmichael shared a joke with the inspector. 'Did you hear about the magician who couldn't pull a rabbit out of his hat?' he asked, a big grin on his face.

'No. Tell me.'

'He pulled a hare out of his bum instead,' replied the sergeant, then looked a bit confused, 'although I don't quite get it. I like hares, with their long ears, but the boys told me it was hysterically funny.'

Falconer smothered a smile. 'And you got that from the boys?'

'I did. Did you want to hear another one?'

'If I must,' answered the inspector.

'Why are pirates called pirates?'

'I don't know, Sergeant. Why are pirates called pirates?'

'Because they are.'

'I think you'll find that "it's because they *arrr*".'

'I don't get that one either.'

'I'll explain them to you one day when you're old enough to understand.'

'Thank you, sir, although I'm sure I could work them out, given time. Jokes were easier in my day.'

'Nice bright boys.'

'Thank you, sir.'

The search party went out again at first light, scouring the countryside round Market Darley for any signs of Natalie Jones.

Falconer and Carmichael met at the station, then drove over in the Boxster to the Mill in Stoney Cross to meet the team who were going to trawl the septic tank. Araminta Wingfield-Heyes and Sadie Palister joined them in the garden as the team arrived.

'When did you last have this emptied, Miss Wingfield-Heyes?' asked the inspector.

'Oh, not for ages, although I did have some drain work done, but it's over a year ago now. I'm here on my own and apparently it's a pretty large tank, so it doesn't need doing very often. I've arranged for the shit truck to pay a visit after you have finished so that I know I'm starting from scratch. The thought of body parts in my cesspit is very unsettling.'

'I'm sure it is, but we have to make sure that it's

not just a spare hand that's been thrown down there no matter how ghoulish that sounds.'

'We're ready to take the top off, sir,' announced one of the team members, and leant down to do so. The big metal cover took a lot of heaving off, but it finally gave way, and a noxious aroma began to pervade the garden.

Carmichael, holding his nose, went over to have a look, suffering from insatiable curiosity, but what he saw was obviously not to his liking, for first he sprayed up his breakfast on to the grass, then he upped feet and laid himself out flat on the lawn.

'You must excuse my sergeant, everybody. He has a weak stomach and is prone to pass out at the slightest thing, or so it would seem.'

'Is that why he's got a bandage on his head? I didn't like to ask before,' said Minty.

'His wife's just given birth to twins, and he decided to watch the births.'

'And he did that when she was in labour?'

'Twice,' replied Falconer, kneeling beside his partner and slapping at his cheeks to bring him round. 'In fact, with the sort of luck he's been having, I'm surprised he didn't try to land on the metal top. I think I'd better get him out of here.'

'You can take him inside if you want.'

'That would be a good idea, then I can come back out here again and see what's brought up – apart from the sergeant's bacon and eggs, that is.'

Having left Carmichael to have a nice lie down on a couch, the inspector went back into the garden to find that various things had floated to the top of the flotsam and jetsam in the tank, apart from the obvious. When he'd ascertained that there were more remains inside, he went in and took his sergeant back to his car so that they could return to the station and open another file.

'Any bets on who this one is?' he asked, as he folded Carmichael into the passenger seat.

'I suppose it would be too much to ask for it to be Suzie Doidge,' he replied groggily.

'Probably. In the meantime, how about we help the search party and take Natalie's photo into all the pubs in the town and see if any of the landlords recognise her. Not every landlord's like George Covington in keeping up with the news.'

'Good idea, sir.'

Before the inspector had even had the chance to settle his cheeks in his chair, however, he was called back up to Chivers' office. 'Have you not got this sorted yet?' the superintendent asked in exasperation.

'It's still early days, considering how many bodies there now are. We've just got back from Stoney Cross after seeing body parts pulled out of a septic tank.'

'How disgusting.' The superintendent made a little moue of distaste. 'Are you trying to tell me there's yet another body?'

'That's right.'

'Well, you need to get your finger out, Inspector. There needs to be a resolution to this. People are getting frightened to go out at night, and I've got the national press on my back,' he moaned, 'in case you hadn't noticed the scrum outside the station.'

He then immediately cheered up by adding, 'In

fact, I'm going on television again this evening to see if I can jog people's memories and give the viewing public an update.' This last piece of news he almost purred, and Falconer could see the hefty feed his ego had had on the fact that he would again have his face plastered across screens all over the country. 'This is turning into a pretty nasty but important case. If you can solve it, it'll be a feather in my, er, your cap.'

Falconer suppressed a smile at this slip, and just agreed. It was the only way to get out of the office: when the man was so taken with his own importance that he'd forgotten that he wanted to give the inspector a bollocking.

When he got back to the office, he found Carmichael waiting for him, but there was no sign of Tomlinson.

'He's left a note, sir.'

'Where is he?'

'It looks like he had the same idea as you. He's gone off with a printed list of pubs in Market Darley, and he's going to start the end that Natalie Jones lived. He's left a suggestion that we should go out and start the other end, and that we would all probably bump into each other in the middle. He says to call him on his mobile if you agree. Damned cheek, leaving a note telling you what to do.'

'That's quite all right, Carmichael. It was a good initiative.'

'But I thought the Uniforms had checked all the pubs.'

'They will have, but you know how unforthcoming publicans can be when someone in uniform turns up. *We* might get a bit more cooperation.'

For most of the afternoon they had no luck; then, in the Royal Oak, the tide turned. The manager had not been on duty when the uniformed boys had come in, but on being shown the photograph, he stared for a moment, then said he did recognise her. He had a good memory for faces. 'She was in here with a small gang of girls. They were drinking tequila slammers at a terrific rate. Then they started to get a bit rowdy and I had to ask them to calm down.

'They did for a while, but they ended up singing "Y Viva España" at a terrific volume and, eventually, I asked them to leave. That would've been about ten thirty.'

'How many more of them were there?'

'There were about five altogether.'

'And you're sure this girl was one of them?'

'Absolutely. In fact, she was the lippiest one of the lot.'

'Did you pick up anything about their plans for after the pub?'

'Most of what they were saying was drivel and giggling, so no, I didn't.'

'That sounds very out of character, from what her mother told us.'

'If you ask me, most young women have one personality for home, and quite another one for when they're out with their friends, drinking.'

The man was very wise. 'Come on, Carmichael. Let's go visit Mrs Jones and ask her who Natalie's friends were. She said she was a very shy girl, but that might not be the absolute truth,

180

and she must have some.'

At the Joneses' house, the mother of the missing girl admitted that Natalie went out very occasionally with some old school friends and assumed that was what she'd done on the night she'd disappeared. 'But I still can't get her on her mobile, and I don't know any of her friends' numbers. They would all be on her mobile which I don't have, and I can't get into her Facebook account. It's password protected,' she informed them, dissolving into tears again, but proving that someone had at least put her right on the correct name for the internet site.

'May I send one of my officers round to collect her computer? I'm sure one of our electronic whizzes can crack the password, and that should help us a lot.'

'You're very welcome, I'm sure: anything that helps to find my little girl.'

'Have you no idea whom she kept in touch with when she left school? Has she got any friends from work?'

'I simply don't know. She didn't go out much, but she spent all her time in her bedroom on Facebook or her phone. I've been thinking, and I don't really know that much about her now she's grown up.'

'We're doing all we can. Let us know if there's any news, and we'll keep you updated, Mrs Jones.'

'At least we've tracked down a sighting,' said Carmichael, as they headed off to the next pub.

'And we can let the super know before he goes on the television tonight. It might jog other people's memories, if there was a group of them. It would seem that, like so many younger people today, she lived a vicarious life; never really seeing or doing anything, just reading or talking about other people's lives. It's a sad reflection of the times we live in that young people shut themselves away like hermits in the cave of their bedrooms and don't really interact anymore.'

'Is that your thought for the day, sir?' asked Carmichael, his head on one side to indicate that he meant to prick his superior officer's balloon of pomposity.

'Carmichael.'

'Yes, sir.'

'Shut up.'

'Sir.' And they both smiled quietly to themselves in acknowledgement of the familiarity in this little exchange.

It was the only luck they had and Tomlinson also came back empty-notebooked, having checked in with them from his mobile. 'Not a dicky bird,' he reported. 'No one at all saw her, but at least we tried.

'We picked up a sighting placing her with a group of young women getting rowdy in the Royal Oak, so at least that's something,' Falconer informed him, and Carmichael smiled as if they'd, somehow, earned a house point. 'I'll just nip upstairs and let Jelly know, so that he can include it in tonight's media extravaganza.'

As soon as he got back to his desk the phone rang, and he was informed that the search party had, indeed, turned up a body covered in branches and rubbish in a ditch. 'Apparently one of the cadaver dogs sniffed it out, but there was no way they could have seen it. So, that's yet another one on our list. We'd better get some suspects fast or we'll be drummed out of the force. Still, I suppose it'll be easier with the other officers helping out on door-to-door. This is turning into a nightmare on a huge scale, according to the media, and I quite agree with them.'

The bones and bits and pieces from the septic tank were duly delivered to Doc Christmas, who almost had a conniption at the filthy state of them and the smell which sneaked into every nook and cranny of his post-mortem room and, to his dismay, his office. His whole suite smelled like a sewer and he realised that even the clothes he wore would have to be at least thoroughly cleaned, if not burned, as well as the whole place fumigated until the vile stench was eliminated.

He called Falconer and announced that he expected him to be present as he examined the disparate parts. Why should he be the only one to suffer with these filthy things? And when the inspector arrived, the medical man smiled behind his mask at the expression of disgust on the detective's face as he entered.

'We haven't quite got it all,' he informed the inspector. 'There are a few bits and pieces missing, but that's not a bad effort your guys have made.'

'I don't think we'll let the owner of the tank know that there might be a few specimens left. She's arranging to have the thing emptied when we're finished with it, and we can then consider, with a clear conscience, that she's free of anymore body parts.'

'It's only the odd finger and toe,' explained the doctor, leading Falconer to a lumpy table covered with a white sheet. 'It was quite a jigsaw that you had delivered to me, though. Any idea who it might be?'

'Not at the moment. Have you any idea how long the parts had been down there?'

'Not with any accuracy. The action of all the microbes and organisms in a septic tank can strip a body in a surprisingly short amount of time, and this was pre-carved, so to speak.'

'How can you be so off-hand?' Falconer winced. 'We're talking about parts of what used to be a living and breathing person, after all.'

'How do you think I face up to my job, Harry boy? If I couldn't look at such things dispassionately, how on earth would I be able to cut up corpse after corpse? I can't allow any emotion into the exercise. You should know better, having been in the army.'

'I'm sorry. I think I shed a lot of the hard carapace I used to wear along with the uniform. Let's get on with this. Is there anything there at all that we might use for identification purposes?'

Doc Christmas flicked off the sheet and exposed a stinking pile of what looked like crap-covered bones. 'Even that giant dog of Carmichael's that you've told me so much about would turn his nose up at this lot,' said the FME as lightly as possible.

Falconer took a deep breath for courage, almost immediately regretting it, and took a good look. 'There's not a lot left, is there?'

'No, but I had a quick peek before you arrived, and I found a couple of gold crowns that might prove more than useful.'

'Can you show me?'

Doc Christmas put out a gloved hand to the skull, and gently moved down the lower jaw bone. 'In there, left, rear.'

'Excellent. Can you get me an x-ray of the teeth, and I'll get them circulated. They shouldn't be too hard to identify.'

'Atta boy, Harry. And by the way, it's a girl.'

'Ad dow I think I'll get back to by teab,' stated Falconer nasally, doing an abrupt about-turn and speeding out of the door, and eventually into clean, fresh, untainted air. Damn, he'd forgotten to pass on a message.

Entering the noisome premises again, he called through to the doctor that there had been a body turned up by the search party, and they would be calling him out to certify death and have a look at it, before it was delivered to him later, then he made off for his car at a trot.

So, they were the remains of a female, were they, that had been taken out of the septic tank? Then this could be the long-missing Suzie Doidge or even the mysteriously disappeared Bonnie Fletcher. Dental records would either disprove or confirm his theory.

He was re-summoned to the post mortem suite again that afternoon when the latest body that had been discovered by the search party had been delivered, as promised, to the FME. It was a mess, having been out in the open for some long time, and the doc wanted Harry Falconer to share in this grim task. If these young women had disappeared while he was in charge of CID, he wanted him to see what had resulted from all these unnoticed disappearances. He knew this was a little unfair, as most of them had not been reported, but he was angry with this pointless loss of life. Maybe he was allowing himself to become involved – always a mistake.

The DI arrived as the doctor was about to start his task, and gagged when he saw the rotted, tattered remains that awaited him. 'My God, Doc, that looks like something from the First World War trenches. How was that never come across before?'

'Oh, it undoubtedly was, but by four-legged creatures rather than those who walk on their hind legs. There have been bits of it nibbled off by animals, I assume, but it was in a ditch that was little frequented by the owner, and Mother Nature's had a good chance to deal with it. Some of the others were in a much better preserved state. I presume you won't be bringing anyone in to identify the body?'

'Ha ha. Very funny. I'm not going to hang around here while you pull that apart because, from the way it looks, you could cut what's left with a butter knife, and I'm feeling decidedly queasy.'

'Wimp!'

'What I will do is arrange for samples to be sent to the lab for DNA testing. We've got hair brushes and toothbrushes and other detritus that should prove perfect for this. What I want you to do is provide samples of what's left of this discovery and get them over to the lab, so that they can do a comparison.

'We should be able to identify the victim from Stoney Cross from the gold crowns. I don't suppose this one has had any esoteric or expensive work done on its teeth?'

'Not so lucky this time, Harry, boy. I had a quick peek, but I'm afraid this poor soul hasn't had many visits from the tooth fairy. DNA's probably your only option. How many girls have you got missing, still?'

'Three,' replied Falconer, 'But one of them is quite a recent disappearance. I think I know who these two are, but not which is which. The sooner we find the dentist who fitted those crowns, the better. Have you got the X-rays done from that skull?'

'Of course I have. I don't hang around, you know.'

'Thanks for your efficiency. I'll get someone going on the dentists and also arrange for an assortment of brushes to be forwarded to the lab if you could prepare tissue samples for them.'

After work that day, DS Carmichael called in to visit his wife and recently born twins, then got himself back to Castle Farthing to see his other three children.

As he opened the door, his mother, who was holding the fort for him at the moment, shouted out, 'Take off your shoes and put your slippers on. I've shampooed the carpets today, and I don't want your enormous boats tracking mud all over them.' She had left his slippers by the door, and he complied, before looking in to see where the children were.

The two boys were sitting at the dining table, apparently doing their homework. Harriet was in her highchair scribbling on a piece of paper with a wax crayon. 'Didn't want them treading on a slightly damp carpet,' his mother explained. 'And don't sit on the suite. I've shampooed that today an' all. Don't know what your Kerry does all day with two of the kids at school. I dropped your Harriet over to Rosemary Wilson so I could get this place bottomed, and it was absolutely filthy.'

Every surface shone, and every window twinkled with cleanliness. OK, Carmichael wouldn't have thought to do housework in the evenings after work, but Mrs Carmichael had got very house-proud since her brood had grown up, and the sergeant remembered the chaos that used to reign in his family home when he was small. She'd certainly changed her tune over the years.

'You never used to be like this,' he challenged her.

'Maybe not, but I had double the kids. Your Kerry's got to do a bit more about the place.' This looked like a declaration of war.

'My Kerry's been carrying twins for months, she's been carrying a lot more weight, as well as dealing with hormones, and we'll live as we please. I don't want to live in a museum or a show house,' her son exploded.

A bit of a yelling match ensued, which had the boys with their hands over their ears and Harriet bawling her eyes out, but eventually they called a truce. Mrs Carmichael senior reflected that she hadn't always been that efficient with the cleaning and tidying, and Carmichael said it was kind of her to have a spring clean for the new mother coming home.

His mother, however, was still top dog where any of her children were concerned. Carmichael found himself unexpectedly in bed at seven thirty, cleared off out of the way with his offspring, so that his mother could shampoo the seats of the dining room chairs and wash the curtains from the lounge. How had that happened?

Falconer had decided, as Honey had turned up on him unexpectedly twice lately, that he would call in at her apartment on the way home. What was sauce for the gander could also be sauce for the goose in his opinion, and he'd surprise her.

He felt an air of excitement as he drove. His transformation had been complete since Honey had been round cherry-hunting, and he'd like a little more of that, if that was all right with his new lover. What a terribly seductive word that was – and he hoped that she would prove to be exactly the same tonight.

The smile on his face froze as he surveyed her expression of absolute horror when she opened the door to him. 'Whatever's the matter?' he asked, a reflex reaction.

'Um, could you possibly go away and come back a little later – say, half an hour?' she asked in an uncertain voice, her eyes wide with trepidation.

'What are you hiding from me? Who's in there?' Falconer's mind filled immediately with anxiety, and he thought the worst: that she was being unfaithful again, and had another man stashed in her bedroom.

'There's nobody in here,' she declared. 'Absolutely nobody at all; except for me.' There was, however, desperation in her voice, and Falconer's suspicions were fully alerted.

'If there's no one in there, why won't you let me in to see?' he asked, perfectly reasonably, although he didn't feel at all reasonable. Surely she couldn't be two-timing him again? After what they had shared together?

'I just can't. But there's nobody else in here. Please don't push it, Harry. Just give me half an hour.'

That was like a red rag to a bull, and Falconer shouldered his way past her and into the apartment, then stopped dead in his tracks as he walked into the living room, utterly appalled at what met his unsuspecting eyes.

When Tomlinson eventually got home, it was to find Imi had gone to work and every work surface in the kitchen, and the small table they ate at, covered in baking – and mess. There were jam tarts, pies, Cornish pasties – his personal favourite – and sponge cakes, along with splatters and dirty bowls and utensils. There was a fruit cake and two Swiss rolls, one vanilla and one chocolate. Had his girlfriend lost her mind – and why was she so messy? Had she become totally addicted to baking and now couldn't stop? Would she have to go to BA – Bakeaholics Anonymous?

Before he could speculate too much further, his eye caught a piece of paper wedged under a tray of scones, and he read it to find that Imi's parents were coming for tea in a couple of days' time, and she'd not be free to do any preparation because of her shifts. She asked if he would mind putting everything in the chest freezer in their spare bedroom, and then she could show them that she was still on the ball, domestically, and hadn't gone to pieces now that he had moved in with her. The note ended with, 'Sorry for the mess. Will clean up when I get back.'

Tomlinson smiled at the way his mind had easily jumped to the worst possible conclusion and, as he casually popped a whole jam tart into his mouth, he grabbed two of the baking trays and set off to put them in to freeze. His girlfriend was not only an enthusiastic baker, but she also efficiently planned ahead. She may be messy, but she acknowledged the fact, and promised to clean up her own chaos. And it showed how much notice he'd taken of the contents of the kitchen cupboards, because he hadn't even known she had possessed so many baking trays. She must have done this sort of mass bake before, when time was short, and something important was on the horizon.

Even though he didn't see much of Imogen, he saw more of her than he had when he had lived in Cornwall, and she made sure that he always had plenty of comfort food to while away any lonely hours, knowing that he never put on an ounce of weight. At least he knew he'd never go short of food in this new life of his, and work was getting pretty interesting, too.

Falconer's face was a mask of absolute horror as he surveyed the state of the living room, the abandoned cups, plates and bowls, and the casual layer of magazines and newspapers that lay all over the floor and tables. When he'd last seen this place it looked like an exhibit for the Ideal Home Exhibition. Now, it was a disaster area. No wonder she'd been the one to call on him unexpectedly recently.

Behind him, he could see Honey with her hands over her face, trying to stifle the sobs that leaked through her fingers.

'What?' he asked in confusion.

'I'm so sorry, Harry. It was a good thing that we didn't usually come here, because I'm not actually very organised, and I spent days clearing up and cleaning before you came round for a meal. I know how fastidious you are, even though I'd only peeked into your house, before you let your hair down, so to speak.'

'I can't spend any time in here,' he declared.

'Don't run out on me again. I'll change,' she pleaded, seeing her chances with this man going from 'just about sorted' to 'binned along with the other rubbish'.

Falconer stood in complete silence, thinking, while Honey waited anxiously. 'You know how intense my job is,' she pleaded, as he still refrained from speaking.

'Please say something – anything. What can I do to convince you that I'll stop living like this? I'm sorry I duped you.'

Finally, the inspector uttered, 'What you can do is you can come back with me now and stay until the morning, then you can get yourself a regular cleaner to come in and keep you in hand. You may be able to change a bit but I don't expect miracles to start with. If you want to live differently, I can only encourage you to make the effort.'

'I need to be organised,' Honey said, rather ruefully, 'And I think, now I've got something to look forward to – you – I can make the necessary alteration to the way I look at my living quarters.'

'Are you sure you want to?' asked Falconer, his fingers crossed behind his back as he awaited her reply.

'I was always very tidy at home, and I wasn't too bad here until we broke up that last time, then I sort of went to pieces.'

'Right, kiddo, get some black bags. This isn't what I envisaged doing this evening, but let's at least have the rubbish bagged and binned, and you can get a domestic in with a relatively clean slate. Let's get going.'

Honey couldn't believe it when she instantly obeyed. This was what she had needed for so long: a strong man to be masculine with her and stop her being a domestic sloven. It was just lack of direction in her domestic life that had made her such a slouch when it came to maintaining decent quarters.

The whole place looked a lot better when they finally finished taking the last bag out to the wheelie bins in the car park, and Falconer had a twinkle in his eye as he slung an arm around her shoulder when they left for his place. She had changed his life completely by introducing him to someone hitherto unindulged in activity. Why shouldn't he be able to change hers by re-educating her about housekeeping? Between them, they should make a pretty good team.

Chapter Fifteen

The inspector arrived at the station on time the next morning, but with bags under his eyes from lack of sleep, and had to fight his way through a jostling crowd of press at the entrance. It had been a pleasurable night, but on top of all the clearing out he had to help with at Honey's apartment, the two of them had not got a lot of sleep, once they had satisfied their appetites in more than one way, a Chinese take-away being the first of these.

During the morning, he received the information that his extra DCs had dealt with the X-rays and now had a name for the dismembered body and had also sent DNA samples from all the victims to the lab and instructed them not only to look for the identity of the body found by the search party, but to see if they could cross-reference them with the handbags found by the metal detectorist. There may have been no fingerprints found on them, but there could easily be identifiable DNA in the creases and folds of the bags.

The report on the dismembered body showed that it was Bonnie Fletcher, Wanda Warwick's dear friend from Shepford St Bernard, and the decomposing body had been that of the long-searched-for Suzie Doidge. At last she'd come to light. Falconer had only two thoughts in his head: to break the news of Bonnie Fletcher's definite

194

demise to those who needed to know – Wanda Warwick and the poor girl's parents – and to work out where a body could possibly have been dismembered. Of course, there was a helluva lot that he didn't know yet, like who was responsible for all these deaths, but he was a patient man.

When he'd broken the news of the most recent victim's death, he could see about finding Natalie Jones and making a new list of suspects, but his brain could only cope with so many tasks at once, and he would have to work within the confines of it.

Falconer decided to go on his own to Shepford St Bernard, as he owed it to Wanda Warwick to tell her of her friend's demise as she had been so tireless in following up whether there had been any sightings or breakthroughs in finding her. He would ask her to keep quiet about his news until he had time to inform her parents, then she could cease her disquieting thoughts about her friend. The worst had happened, and there was nothing they could do to change that.

She opened the front door of her home, Ace of Cups, and immediately discerned from his sombre face that the news he brought was not good. 'You've found her, haven't you?' she almost whispered. 'And she's dead, isn't she?'

'I'm so sorry not to have brought better news, but yes, we have recovered Ms Fletcher's body in the course of our enquiries,' he replied.

'Can I ask where she was found, and whether she suffered?'

It was a quite natural question, although the second part of it would probably never be answered. The inspector did his best to answer the first half, hoping that she wouldn't notice he hadn't supplied any information about the second. 'It will be in the newspapers and on the television news soon enough, so I might as well tell you. You must promise, however, not to say anything to another living soul until I've had time to talk to her parents.' That was the stuff to give the troops.

'I give you my word. Just tell me how long to wait. I think I might be in need of a shoulder to cry on before long.' Long held-back tears were already tracking down her cheeks as she awaited news that she knew would distress her. How could it not? Her friend was dead.

'I think we ought to sit down first,' Falconer advised her. 'It's not very pleasant.'

Wanda Warwick almost fell into an armchair and sat there looking at him plaintively as he took a seat opposite her. As he began to speak, she reached a hand out blindly for tissues from a box on the table beside her.

'I'm afraid your friend's body was found in a septic tank in Stoney Cross. There's no easy way to tell you this, Ms Warwick, but it appears she was dismembered before her body was disposed of. Her remains only came to light when part of her anatomy appeared most unexpectedly, but I can assure you that her remains have been gathered together and she will be able to have a proper burial.' That was more than enough detail to keep her distracted from any suffering that might have been caused, he hoped.

Wanda Warwick's shoulders shook with emotion,

196

as did her hands, from shock. 'And she was actually cut up?'

'I'm very much afraid so.'

'They didn't start before she was dead, did they?' she squeaked in horror, picking up on the only point that he had hoped she would miss.

'There is absolutely no evidence to demonstrate that she wasn't completely dead before she was ... cut up,' he reassured her – and this was indeed true, although he'd have to speak to Doc Christmas to see if there were any marks on the bones to indicate how she had died.

The poor woman collapsed into sobs, and rolled her body into a ball. 'Oh my God! Oh my God! Who would do that to another person? And why Bonnie?'

'That's what my colleagues and I are attempting to find out. She was evidently part of the killing spree that has been making headlines in the papers, and we intend to find whoever is responsible and prosecute them to the full extent of the law.'

'Why don't they bring back hanging?' came as a strangled cry from the balled-up woman in the chair.

Falconer, with his new, reformed character as one who did not recoil from physical contact, got to his feet, and put an arm around the woman's shaking shoulders. 'Just give me half an hour or so after I leave here, and then you can call on a friend or relative who might help to calm you, or at least give you a shoulder to cry on. In fact, Wanda, I'll phone you after I've visited her parents to let you know they've been informed. Then you can talk to

197

whomsoever you please.'

He left her crying openly and was glad that he wasn't headed back to the police station, because it had been awash with press ever since news had leaked about the body discovered by the search party. It was practically under siege by the press and by TV vans and reporters.

Mr and Mrs Fletcher were devastated to know about their daughter's death. They had grown used to Bonnie not living at home, and Mrs Fletcher said that, as far as she was concerned, she would just think of her daughter as living abroad. That would be enough comfort for her until she had got used to the idea that the child they had borne and brought up was no longer on this earth.

Five murders, thought Falconer as he headed back to his desk and his team. How had they ended up with five murders uncovered in such a short time? He'd have to look at the disappearance dates and see if there was any specific timing between the murders. And what was the link between the victims? Why had they been selected, or was it just random? And who the hell was responsible? He'd have to consider his suspect list again and go through theories with his team.

The search had not revealed any trace of Natalie Jones. He would have to see about following up that tip-off from the landlord of the Royal Oak, but just as he sat down in his office chair, he had a telephone call from Ida Jones, telling him, a little shamefacedly, that she had just received a post-card from her daughter, postmarked Spain.

It explained in as few words as possible that she had jetted off, on a whim, with a few old schoolfriends that were going on holiday together. She had had her passport in her bag, and they had managed to get her a seat on the plane. Unfortunately, she had left her mobile in her friend's house in Market Darley, had still been rather inebriated the morning of their departure, and had acted completely without thought. She hoped her mother had not been worrying too much, and she was sorry she couldn't ring her, as her friends didn't have 'roaming' on their phones, which were all pay as you go. It ended with 'see you next weekend. Sorry if you've been upset. Just needed a little holiday.'

'I'm ever so embarrassed,' she explained. 'And you've gone to all that trouble and expense, not to mention police time, mounting that search party. I don't know how to apologise enough for the trouble I've caused.'

'That's what we're here for,' Falconer comforted the distraught woman through gritted teeth, thinking that if they hadn't had the search party they'd never have found what remained of Suzie Doidge, and her disappearance would have gone on haunting him. And he could really blame the superintendent for the attention they had eventually given the supposed disappearance. His first hunch that she had gone off with a man may have been wrong, but he hadn't been far off track.

That group of old schoolfriends must have been the girls she had been seen with in the Royal Oak, and the fact that they were downing tequila slammers at no slow rate must have been the reason she acted so impulsively. She must be having a good time, otherwise she would have contacted home sooner. Little minx. Still, it was one less young woman to worry about – and he wouldn't get a huge bollocking, not if old Jelly had any sense of decency, because it was really the super's wife who had set this particular ball rolling downhill.

Not that he shouldn't have been worried about the girl's apparent disappearance. Call it a gut instinct – call it distraction by Honey, if he was really honest – he simply wasn't doing his job as meticulously as he should have been. He'd have to stay late tonight and try to establish a thread that connected the victims.

'OK, everyone,' he said, calling the team to attention, for they were now situated in one of the meeting rooms, with the expanded team. 'Natalie Jones has been discovered alive and well, and holidaying in Spain without her mobile, but why she had her passport with her, I simply can't fathom – unless she had already booked the holiday, of course. Apparently she just went off on a whim, but I've the feeling that was just a white lie for her mother. Whatever the truth is, she's not on our books anymore as a missing person.'

'What we have to look at is those who were murdered and whose deaths are still unsolved. Three of our victims were without family or close friends, and didn't work full-time: Annie Symons, Suzie Doidge, and Marilyn Slade. Melanie Saunders occasionally took live-in jobs, and Bonnie Fletcher didn't have a wide circle of friends.

'What I need you to do is scour the internet and any other records available to you – use the brains that the good God gave you – and try to find any connection between these young women. Dig up whether they ever belonged to any society or club. Were they regulars anywhere to eat, to drink, or even to change their library books? With whom have they had relationships that broke up? Something must have driven some of them into their shells, for none of them seems to have had a regular boyfriend. This is going to be a massive digging operation, and I want you to get out your spades. Discount nothing.'

Dragging a blank piece of paper over, the inspector began to make a list. They had a last-worked date for Suzie Doidge for Easter 2009. They had a date of 17 May 2009 as the last shift worked by Annie Symons. Marilyn Slade had not been into the craft shop since January 2010 – Amy Littlemore had finally uncovered this from her scrappy staff records. Jefferson Grammaticus had had a missed meeting with a prospective member of staff, Melanie Saunders, in May 2010 – and where was that dratted list of workmen that the man had promised faithfully to supply? Bonnie Fletcher had gone missing in February 2011, a year ago now. Was there any connection between these dates?

There had been two in the very early stages of the spree, only a month apart. Then there had been a gap of eight months, then a gap of only five months. The final gap was seven months, and then nothing for a year. Was this a true timetable, or were there still more horrors to come to light? Why was there that apparent respite at the end? Why had the murders seemed to have stopped?

What were the methods of killing the first two? The first body found, Annie Symons, had been stabbed in the chest. There had been evidence of a chipped rib. The second, Melanie Saunders, had had her throat cut; what about the other three victims? He'd better phone Philip Christmas and try to get his head straight.

'Hello, Harry. I was just compiling a round-up report for you,' the cheerful voice of the doctor sounded in the inspector's ear.

'What have you got for me?'

'Did you get my report on Marilyn Slade? Probably knifed in the left side, in the back.'

'Not so sure I did' – there would be questions asked about this. 'What about the latest two?'

'Suzie Doidge was probably garrotted, judging from the remains of the tissues round the neck. And Bonnie Fletcher, I really have no firm idea about. Although there is evidence of some blunt force trauma to the back of the skull, I can't say for certain that this was what killed her or whether it happened post-mortem. The dismemberment wasn't exactly carried out by an expert, and there are so many nicks on so many bones, that I hardly know where to start.'

'But she was dead when the bastard started?'

'We can only presume so, there being very little left of her for me to examine.'

'This is most unusual, the different *modus operandi* each time. It's rare that a multiple killer employs different means. Repeated crimes usually show some correlation of method.'

'Maybe whoever this is is just creative, or they used what was to hand on each occasion.'

'I suppose so, but it's still rare to have different MOs.'

'Then you either have someone with a very unusual mind, Harry, my boy, or you've got more than one killer.'

'Don't say that! I'm having enough trouble as it is. I think I'm going to have to consult the psychiatric skills of Dr Dubois on this,' Falconer concluded, a smile curving his lips. That would certainly be a pleasure.

When he'd ended the call he asked Carmichael to follow up on the addresses discovered with the children's book manuscript found in Annie Symons' belongings, and to make sure that the team pressed forward in finding the facts about the barmaid who was said to have gone missing from the Covingtons' last pub in London. 'And don't take no for an answer,' he stated emphatically, knowing that was exactly what he'd done when he had tried to follow this up.

He then got in touch with the Forensic Department to see if they'd managed to uncover any DNA from the five handbags that had been dug up, and whether they had been matched to the victims.

'God, you're impatient, aren't you?' answered a technician when he phoned, and Falconer felt a little tempted to pull rank. 'But we should have some results for you in the morning. If you can wait that long.' The inspector canned his negative thoughts, kept his mouth shut, and thanked the man. He didn't want to rile anyone in that department. It could cause a whole bundle of inefficiency and delay in the future. Always best to stay on the good side of anyone on the technical staff. They could either rush your stuff through or accidentally misplace it for days.

'That would be very much appreciated,' he finally managed to choke out before pressing the button that finished the call.

Carmichael finished his calls to publishers before the end of his working day, and reported that none of those listed had received an unsolicited manuscript from anyone by the name of Annie Symons. All of them had stated that they did not accept unsolicited works in any case, and merely sent them back when they arrived.

By the time he was ready to go home, Falconer had also compiled a list of all the possible suspects that they had, and planned to discuss the possibilities of how they could be murderers with Honey this evening. He'd just given her a ring and explained his difficult situation to her, and she'd agreed that she might be able to help him towards a more creative killer if he told her something about each one.

She also said that she'd been able to engage a regular cleaner – at great expense – and asked if they could meet at his place; a suggestion that he readily agreed to, already fighting to keep his mind on his suspects. This wouldn't do at all. Just as his private life had moved from limbo to heaven, his working life had gone to hell in a handcart. He really needed to find a happy medium.

Seven o'clock came and went, as did half past, and when the clock crept round to eight o'clock, he began to get worried. Where had Honey got to? Had she had an accident on the way over? Where was she?

As he got his mobile out of his jacket pocket, he remembered that he'd turned it to silent before he left the office as he hadn't wanted to be disturbed. There was a message on it. His beloved had been summoned to an emergency to deal with a patient who had become psychotic, and she wouldn't be able to make it at all. Perhaps they could rearrange for the following evening. Damn, blast, bugger, and bum, he thought.

Well, in that case, he'd spent his *lonely* evening polishing up his list of suspects, and seeing how there could be any connection between them and all of his victims. He didn't really want to face the idea that there was more than one undetected killer on the loose.

Chapter Sixteen

The forensic results from the excavated handbags were indeed ready the next day, but they weren't at all what Falconer had been expecting. After skimming through them he called out for the rest of the team to stop and pay attention. 'Listen up!' he called, clapping his hands to silence the buzz of conversation that filled the meeting room which served as their temporary office.

'I've got the results from Forensics about those handbags, and they read as follows: Annie Symons' DNA sample was matched to the denim bag, Marilyn Slade's was matched to the red fake-crocodile affair, the rather better-quality brown leather bag belonged to Melanie Saunders, and the pink plastic one was Suzie Doidge's. The really surprising thing was that there was no DNA match with any of them for Bonnie Fletcher.'

'So, what about the fifth bag, then?' Tomlinson asked, having a personal interest, as he had been there when they were first unearthed.

'Would you believe that the DNA from that was from someone completely unknown to us?'

'What does that mean, then, sir?' one of the DCs asked, a note of dread in his voice.

'It could mean that we've got another body out there,' Falconer replied with a gallows smile.

'And what about Bonnie Fletcher's handbag?' asked Carmichael.

'Who knows? She may not have had one with her when she went missing, or it could be anywhere. Any ideas, come and talk to me.' Falconer was now totally flummoxed. Carmichael had a good point. Where was Bonnie Fletcher's handbag, assuming she had had one – and what woman would go anywhere without her trusty receptacle? – and why had it not been with the other ones? And whose was the green suede bag? Was there yet another corpse lurking underground somewhere on his patch, just waiting to be found? Another grim thought struck him then: why was there a gap of a year since the last known killing? Surely murderers didn't go away for extended holidays?

While his mind was thus floundering, he had a call from the computer geek who had been assigned to Natalie Jones' computer, and the man was impossible to interrupt. 'That was quite a girl, the one that owned that computer. She was into all sorts on the internet, and the conversations on Facebook would make a whore blush. Someone told me her mother said she was a shy, retiring little flower, but not according to her emails. I'll grant you that all the "doing" seemed to be carried out by her friends, but this little madam was quite a voyeur. Whatever her friends did, she wanted to know in great detail – the whole nine yards. I could hardly believe what I was reading.

'And as for the sites she looked at, she only just stayed this side of prosecution, the stuff they showed. If her mother knew what was going through her little darling's mind she'd blow a fuse...'

Finally, Falconer managed to yell, 'Stop!' halting the whole office. 'I'm afraid I should have called you off. The girl's turned up, safe and well in Spain.'

'You do surprise me. I'd have thought it would be in an alleyway somewhere, if she'd ever acted out some of her fantasies, and...'

'The case is closed. Please leave the machine where it can be collected by a uniformed officer and returned to its owner, or at least her mother.' The inspector abruptly ended the call before the caller blew out his earwax. There was a man who was keen on his job, and he wondered, suddenly, what the technician had on *his* laptop. Had he perhaps come across some old favourites?

'Sir, did we have all the girls' personal stuff brought back to the evidence room?' asked Carmichael in the convenient silence.

'We did, causing some problems, there's so much of it.'

'Would you mind if I just went and had a riffle through it. You never know what you're going to turn up when you look at something with fresh eyes.'

'Be my guest, Sergeant. Any new discovery would be greatly appreciated.'

Carmichael didn't return to the office for over an hour, but when he did re-enter it, he was waving a newspaper aloft, an expression of triumph on his face. 'Got something here, sir. We just didn't think to look there before,' he almost yodelled.

'Is that the *Carsfold Gazette* you're waving around?'

'It is, sir, and look at this, circled in the lonely hearts column. "AS of Castle Farthing, looking for creative male, 25-40. GSOH. No strings. No children. Must be sensitive and affectionate". It's even got a phone number listed.'

'Do you reckon that's our Annie Symons?'

'I did get it from one of the boxes we collected from the corner shop.' Carmichael was clearly delighted with himself. 'And I bet she got some funny calls. Why on earth do you think she put her real telephone number in?'

'Naïveté?' suggested Falconer.

'Living dangerously?' asked Tomlinson.

'I think it was probably sheer innocence. None of the evidence about her suggests that she would welcome being inundated by phone calls from weirdos,' countered Carmichael, indicating that he was a bit more with it and more up to speed.

'Can one of you check out the number in the ad

while I phone the editor of the paper?' Falconer requested.

David Porter himself answered the ringing phone and greeted Falconer like an old friend. 'You've really got us run off our feet,' he said. 'Nothing like this has ever happened round here before, and we've never had so much news to report. Keep up the good work.'

'I sincerely hope not, if that's counted in corpses.'

'Sorry, that was in rather dubious taste. What exactly can I do for you?'

'Your lonely hearts column.'

'What about it?' The editor's curiosity was definitely piqued.

'You had an advert in it in your edition dated – hang on a minute. What was the date of that newspaper, Carmichael? – 8th May, 2009, from an AS of Castle Farthing. We think that might be one of our victims, but I want you to keep schtum about that and what I'm about to ask you – if you do I'll give you a scoop on it.'

'What is it you want me to do?'

'Check through editions since then for these names: Melanie Saunders, Suzie Doidge, Marilyn Slade, and Bonnie Fletcher. That's the women I need to check up on. As far as men go, I'd like you to check if adverts have been placed by any of the following: Timothy Driscoll, Colin Bridger, Michael Mortimer, Simeon Perkins, and George Covington.'

There was a large sigh at the other end of the phone. 'And Uncle Tom Cobbley and all, I suppose. You're just lucky I've got a work experience kid in at the moment, and I can spin any sort of excuse I like to justify such a search. Of course, you do realise that people don't always use real names in these things, and sometimes, as you've discovered, just initials?'

'Then that will just add extra delight to whoever is under your watchful eye for their time in work experience, won't it?'

'This could take some time,' Porter said, with a touch of acid in his voice.

'It'd be worth it, though, for a scoop, wouldn't it?'

'You blackmailing bastard, Harry.'

'That's me. Get back to me if you get any results.'

'This had better be worth it,' concluded the editor, ending the call with another audible sigh.

About half an hour later he had an internal call from Bob Bryant. 'I've got a couple down at the desk come to hand in a handbag they've found. It's in pretty poor shape, so it doesn't look like it might have been mislaid yesterday, but they say there's a Yale key in a little side pocket, so they thought someone might have missed it. I understand that you're the "handbag man of the moment".'

'Cheeky swine,' Falconer hissed, then raising his voice to its normal level, 'I'll come right down. I could do with stretching my legs. Pop them into an interview room until I get there.'

'Will do. Thanks, Inspector.'

In interview room two he found what appeared to be a retired couple who introduced themselves as Mr and Mrs Greenacre. 'We've handed in that handbag we found to that nice sergeant at the desk,' Mrs Greenacre informed him.

'That's very public-spirited of you. Thank you very much. Could you tell me how and where you found it, please?'

'We're keen walkers, now we don't work anymore. We like to keep fit, avoid the old man with the scythe and all that jazz,' rambled her husband.

'Anyway,' she cut in, 'We were having a little stroll out in that wooded section near Coldwater Pryors, and we saw the bag in a bramble bush.'

'Not that it was easy to see, mind you. It was with it being winter and all that, and there being no leaves on it, that we could see it at all.'

'There were still plenty of thorns,' the woman informed Falconer. 'It was me that fished it out. Look at my hands,' she instructed him, holding them out to display a number of scratches.

'I told you not to take those gloves out of your coat pocket this early in the year.'

'But it was milder today.'

Falconer cleared his throat. He didn't want this simple story to turn into a domestic. 'And you looked inside it, did you?'

'That's right.' Mr Greenacre now took up the tale again. 'There was nothing in the main body of the bag, but the wife noticed a little, almost concealed, pocket on the thin edge. She's got right good eyesight, has the wife.'

'And you looked inside that, did you?' This was looking like it could turn into the verbal equivalent of pulling teeth.

'That's right, Inspector, we did. And there was

211

this door key. Your desk sergeant took that as well.'

'Did you just look, or did you take it out?'

'Oh, we took it out to see if there was anything underneath it.' So that made fingerprints more difficult then, the inspector thought wryly. But maybe this was the missing handbag of Bonnie Fletcher that had not been with the main cache?

'If I got an officer to return with you to the area, could you identify exactly where you found it?'

'Absolutely,' the husband reassured him.

While one of the DCs took them away to identify the scene of the find, Falconer got the handbag sent off for DNA testing, and took the key himself. He had a good idea where this fitted, and he wanted to test his theory.

Leaving a message with Bob Bryant about where he was headed in case anyone needed him, he drove out to Shepford St Bernard. The key fitted perfectly into the lock on the front door of Robin's Perch. It was Bonnie Fletcher's bag after all, so that was that little mystery solved. He was right that no woman would go anywhere without her cosmetics and comb.

But, where had the cache come from? Why had this one been dumped somewhere different, and to whom did the stray bag belong? These and many other questions whirled in his mind, but the main one was, what on earth was the connection between the five – possibly six – victims?

They ranged from mid-twenties to early thirties, but this was all they seemed to have in common, although there must be a connecting factor. It was his job to find out what that was. He decided to corral his regular partners in their old office when he got back, and see if they could come up with something. The three of them had developed a kind of professional bond that he did not feel yet with the recently arrived DCs from other forces, and he would find it difficult to open himself up with such a large group.

On his return, he checked that Carmichael and Tomlinson were in the old meeting room and then slipped upstairs to where they had worked so harmoniously together for quite a while. In fact, it seemed as if Tomlinson had been there a lot longer than he had. He was an easy-going man with whom it was not difficult to get on, as long as he stopped his eulogies on his home county and didn't have the bare-faced cheek to refer to the inspector again as 'me old lover'. Collecting three chairs from the corridor, he placed them in the middle of their old space and slipped downstairs again to fetch the officers. If they could talk it through a bit, and he could have a professional chat with Honey this evening – together with AOB! – he might get somewhere.

As he put his head round the door, he heard the Market Darley DC's voice sounding above the buzz of other voices. 'And you should see the coast at Tintagel. It's just breathtaking.'

'Carmichael. Tomlinson. With me, now,' he barked to get their attention and, as they mounted the stairs, he tackled the first of his bugbears. 'Tomlinson, do you think you could quit the "Look at Life" you do on your native county? We understand it's a very beautiful area, but so is this, and we don't go on all the time extolling its

213

virtues, do we? If we've never seen the Cornish countryside, I'm sure we'll go and have a look one day. If we have, you're probably preaching to the converted, and it can be a little bit of a strain.'

'Sorry, sir. I'll try to keep a lid on it. It's just that I miss it so much.'

'Then take some of your free time and have a drive through our highways, byways, and villages. I'm sure you'll find a similar level of beauty, but just in a less dramatic way. This is really a lovely area, if you take the time to explore it. When the weather improves, take your girlfriend on some picnics. You'll find yourself pleasantly surprised. For instance, have you ever examined the ancient castle ruins just to the north of the village where Carmichael lives?'

'I didn't even notice them when I went there,' the DC admitted.

'I expect your mind was on what you intended to do once you arrived. Take a while and just walk round them. They're lovely.'

'They are that,' confirmed the DS. 'Sometimes I take the dogs there instead of into the woods. They love chasing round the old lumps of stone and the crumbling walls. And there're some really lovely remains of thirteenth-century gothic windows.'

'Thanks for the tip,' replied Tomlinson. It hadn't occurred to him that he hadn't really given the area a chance to shine, and he had certainly found the village of Castle Farthing picturesque. 'We'll start there and work our way outwards, me old lover.'

Falconer was not sure to which of them this remark was addressed, but immediately jumped on it, as it was his only other source of annoyance with this officer. 'And around here, we don't refer to anyone as "me old lover", let alone superior officers. Surnames or ranks will be fine in the workplace. Anything else will be by personal arrangement with that individual. OK?'

'Sorry about that. Old Cornish habit,' replied the constable, and then blushed as he realised he had mentioned his home county yet again.

Once sat in the bare office on the plain wooden chairs, Falconer asked them if they had any theories on why the victims had been chosen or who might have killed them.

Carmichael was the first to offer up anything. 'We sort of know it wasn't promiscuity. The only one who seemed a bit that way was Suzie Doidge, because the woman in the other flat said she was a bit of a goer.'

'The only visitor to Annie Symons' address we can be sure of is Colin Bridger with this daft tale about writing a children's story together,' chipped in Tomlinson.

'Although we do have the manuscript to prove it was written,' Falconer counselled them with caution, 'albeit there is no evidence to confirm that they had compiled it as a joint effort.'

'It could've been just a smokescreen for whatever else was going on,' suggested the DC. 'And Marilyn Shade didn't seem to socialise much.'

'Bonnie Fletcher was going out on a date the night she disappeared. Have we found out who that was with yet? I know she was very cagey with Ms Warwick.' It was Falconer's turn to add something.

'And that Melanie Saunders was applying for a live-in job,' ventured Carmichael. 'If she'd had any of those in the past, then we need to get someone on to her employment record to see if she might have been having flings with male members of staff.'

'Or even female members,' added the inspector daringly, smiling at Carmichael's distressed face at the very idea. 'But, good idea, Sergeant. Now, what about the possible killers? Let's start with George Covington.'

'A bit unlikely, isn't he, sir?' asked Carmichael. 'I mean, he's been at The Fisherman's Flies for years, and he's never looked at all menacing to me.'

'You're not a young, attractive woman, are you? That makes a difference.'

'But surely he's too old,' opined Tomlinson with the callowness of youth.

'On the contrary, I've been told you're never too old,' Falconer advised him, simply to be contrary. 'I shall let you know about that when I hit eighty,' he added, with unusual levity. Looking at his watch, he suddenly gasped. 'Good Lord, look at the time. I'd completely lost touch with it. I'm expecting a visitor tonight, and I'm sure you two have things to do too. Put your thinking caps on, and we'll have another chat tomorrow. I'm just sorry that this session couldn't last longer.'

At this, the inspector jumped to his feet and made a hasty exit, rubbing his hands together with glee. 'Whatever's got into him, Neil?' asked Carmichael. 'I know he's been acting a bit strangely lately. I have, myself, but my wife's just given birth

216

to twins, and that's only to be expected. But, what's eating him? I've never known him like this before.'

'Methinks our revered senior officer is, perhaps, getting his leg over, Davey,' suggested Tomlinson, also taking the opportunity to slip on to first name terms.

'No! Never! He simply wouldn't do that.' Carmichael was scandalised, but did not object to the use of his forename, especially as it wasn't the one he had been given at his baptism.

'And who exactly was this visitor he was so anxious to get home to?' Tomlinson wasn't giving up that easily.

'Surely not Dr Honey Dubois? I thought he was going to give that a rest while he concentrated on this case.'

'Did you actually believe him when he came in a couple of hours late the other morning, and claimed he had forgotten to tell us about a dental appointment?'

'I don't believe I was in that day – but it's impossible that he would have had an appointment and not have told us about it in advance, or at least rung in,' Carmichael agreed.

'And have you seen that smug smile on his face when he thinks nobody's looking?'

'I have noticed he seems rather more cheerful, but I thought that that was maybe me thinking that the whole world was happy at the moment. I have been a bit out of it.'

'You couldn't help that, Davey. By the way, have you and your wife settled on any names yet for your new additions?'

'It would seem that Persephone and Apollo are the flavours of the month with Kerry.'

'Blimey! How has she managed to swing that one?'

'By reminding me of the other first names in my family. You don't want to know, although I'll let you into a little secret: my given names are actually Ralph and Orsino. I'm Davey by choice.'

'How could you possibly disagree with her, with monikers like that? So, to round things off, do you think the old man's on the nest?'

Although bristling at that way of referring to what was, in fact, their senior officer, Carmichael had to agree that there were certainly signs that something was afoot to make him that happy.

'I'll mention cherries tomorrow, and see if he owns up to admitting that he doesn't have one anymore,' said the irrepressible DC with an impish grin that would have done justice to a Cornish piskie.

'You wouldn't dare.'

'You just wait and see.'

'We didn't come to any conclusions in our little meeting did we?' Carmichael stated lugubriously.

'That's because we weren't as alluring as the person I have heard referred to in the canteen as "the delicious coffee-coloured shrink". By the way,' he continued, as Carmichael gasped at the man's impertinence, 'has anyone checked whether Driscoll or Bridger own any other properties, or might have, in the last three or four years? Also, have any other of our victims lived in the properties they now own, or may have owned? For all we know they could both own a whole string of properties, and our victims have just been going around renting them for years. I know that sounds a bit muddly, but you get my gist, Davey.'

'I think I see what you're getting at, Neil. I'll talk it over with the team tomorrow morning, and see if we can't sort out how to get our hands on the information about properties, bought, owned or sold in the relevant period, by those two. Have a nice evening. I'm going off to visit Kerry and the twins, now.'

'Give her my best,' called Tomlinson after the figure of the retreating giant.

Carmichael had one jaw-dropping conversation after another. When he got to Kerry's bedside, she explained that it was very lucky that the twins had been born early. If her pregnancy had gone to full term, she would not have been able to deliver them naturally. As she had already had three children, she would probably not have got to her due date anyway, and the whole thing could have ended up in an emergency caesarean section.

'Anything could have happened, Davey,' she told him in a concerned voice. 'They were so big because of your build. They'd have been absolute monsters if I'd gone on much longer, and this was my body's way of doing its best for them – Harriet must take after me. They also think I got my dates a bit wrong, and that the pregnancy was further advanced than we'd thought. That's why they didn't need to go into incubators or anything like that.

'The doctor told me that we were very lucky that things happened exactly as they did. We got the best possible outcome: healthy mother without stitches, and two healthy babies, not too light. It shouldn't be too long before all three of us can come home. I'm so looking forward to it.'

'So am I. Do you know my mother sent me to bed one night with the children so that she could shampoo the dining chairs? She's shampooed, washed and cleaned everything that isn't nailed down, and quite a few things that actually are.'

Kerry knew Mrs Carmichael senior quite well, and she wasn't surprised. 'Never mind, Davey, we'll soon get it feeling like home again.'

'Thank God for that. At the moment, it's like living inside an advert for cleaning products. It all seems so antiseptic.'

'Maybe I'll get like that when all the kids leave home.'

'Promise me you won't.'

Chapter Seventeen

When Falconer got home that night, he got out the vacuum cleaner, and the duster and polish, and just gave everything a quick going over. He didn't want Honey catching him out on the housework stakes; not after he'd given her such a thorough talking-to the night before. She arrived as he was swilling a bleachy cloth round the sink, and he dried his hands, and walked out of the kitchen to let her in. There was a lot of talking he wanted them to do before anything else reared its delightful head. No, no, don't think like that, he thought, as the inevitable started to happen.

'Come on in,' he invited her, putting his baser feelings into an emotional freezer. He really needed to pick her professional brains, rather than indulge in another session of appreciating her body. 'Let me get you a glass of wine and pour out all my troubles. I need your cool, analytical mind on some pretty rum coves.'

'Should I restrict my wine intake?' she asked innocently.

'Why?'

'In case I have to drive later.'

'Oh, I don't think there's any chance of that, do you?'

Taking a goodly swig of wine, she smiled at him and told him to pour out his heart before he poured her anything else.

'I've got five suspects,' he began. 'I've also got five corpses. I think one of the former is responsible for all of the latter, but I can't understand why there were so many different methods of killing.'

'OK, first, tell me about your suspects,' she prompted him.

'Right, let's start with George Covington. He's landlord of The Fisherman's Flies pub in Castle Farthing. He's about sixty, married, and has worked in a pub in London before. He seems a very genial mine host and quite harmless. Yet he knew all the victims, and his wife has mentioned that a barmaid disappeared from their last pub in the capital. By the way, two of the victims worked the odd shift for him.'

'That's number one,' she responded. 'Now give me a potted history of number two.'

'Colin Bridger,' Falconer began, almost like a declaration. 'He's the owner of one of the victim's properties. He also claims to have collaborated on a book of fairy stories with her. It sounds like a load of codswallop, but we actually have a draft of the book in our possession. He used to visit her regularly, supposedly to work on the book. He's not a young man – he's retired, though it was early retirement, from managing a plant nursery – and he's married. Seems a bit afraid of his wife. One grown-up daughter. I've got some information on their backgrounds from my expanded team. You can look at my notes later – among other things.' He gave her a leery wink and she sniggered.

'Check, two,' confirmed Honey.

'Then we have another property owner, Timothy Driscoll, whom we thought lived in France, but it turned out he'd only been there for a year. He still uses a French mobile and lives a bit of a reclusive life. He's not married, used to live with a girlfriend, but that broke up, and he made a botch-up of his attempt at a new start in France. Doesn't like being seen as a failure. Currently unemployed. Used to work for the local authority, but at the moment is at a loose end.

'We've also got two men of alike occupation – both general builders and handymen. We'll start with Michael Mortimer. He lives four doors from victim number one. He says he only knew her to nod to. Does the occasional bigger job with his neighbour, Simeon Perkins, who's my final suspect. Both are unmarried. As an aside, Mortimer has a passing resemblance to the Hunchback of Notre Dame, so I'm not surprised he's single and lives alone. Of course, I wouldn't be so unprofessional as to make comments like that in the station.

'Simeon Perkins is probably the other side of the coin. General builder again. Tall, blond, and probably quite good-looking if you're a woman, although I can't say that I fancy him.' At this facetious comment he smiled shyly at Honey, who took his hand and squeezed it.

'I'm very glad to hear that, Harry Falconer. I wouldn't be here if I thought any differently.'

The inspector knew he wasn't very good at this flirting business, but he'd have to get used to it gradually. It certainly didn't come as second nature to him, as it did to a lot of men.

'The only thing I can really say about this man is that he doesn't seem to like being interviewed by the police. He lives alone at the moment, but I'm not sure whether he's ever lived with a wife or partner. I'll have to find out.'

'You show me someone who does like being interrogated in a police station.'

Falconer made a harrumphing noise. 'He says he was on greeting terms with the first victim, and, as with Mortimer, he's not married. So, what do you think?'

'I'll give you my opinion for what it's worth. You've got two general builders who also do odd jobs. What does that tell me about them?'

'Don't know.'

'That they're used to turning their hand to different things. They can tackle just about anything in the house-building or maintenance area. They're multi-taskers.

'Then you have two property owners. Ditto, as they probably have to keep an eye on their houses, and I'm sure they must have had to take time renovating or furnishing a property, or even just getting the garden sorted out.'

'True, true.'

'Then you've got a pub landlord – the ultimate multi-tasker. He's got to order and stock his pub, open it and run it, and keep the customers happy. How many skills does that take? And maybe he's at an age where he's going through a period of crisis about growing old and unattractive.'

'I'm beginning to see what you mean.'

'You mentioned a mixture of methods of killing. Well, none of these men actually works on an assembly line or on a check-out. They all do something that needs a number of different skills. Maybe they just like varying the method to keep their experiences fresh. God, what a horrible thought.'

'But why would they kill at all?'

'Anger, frustration. There are any number of reasons. Some men kill for sexual pleasure. Have you thought about that one?'

'It's a pretty grim thought, isn't it?'

'But not unknown.'

'And this is a pretty grim case. If I could get a request OKed, would you sit in on the interviews?'

'If permission is granted. But, apart from this pub landlord, have you worked out how any of the other men could know all of the victims?'

'Um, no. Perhaps we're barking up completely

the wrong tree.'

'Your instinct isn't usually that wrong, is it?'

'The only hunch I've had recently is on Mortimer's back.'

'Ha ha. He's not really a hunchback, is he?'

'No, just a bit on the un-pretty side.'

'And you've also got to consider, if the same man murdered all of them, perhaps he was just looking for a bigger thrill by varying the methods of killing.'

'There are some twisted buggers out there, aren't there?'

'Too right there are. And you watch your language, Mr Inspector, otherwise I shall have to spank you.'

'Is that a promise?' asked Falconer.

'You bet your sweet ass it is. Come on. And, by the way, just going back to the prosaic for a second,' she continued, as they mounted the stairs, 'your best bet would be to look at the ones who aren't currently married, and have never, or at least not for a long time, maintained a live-in relationship. You're more likely to find your deviant there.'

'Maybe. Hang on, I haven't told you about the gaps between the deaths!' This really was dedication to duty. They sat on the bed and Falconer explained that there had been an apparent cessation of killings for a period of a year, and about the handbags that had been recovered.

Honey sighed in frustration and made mock-strangling motions with her hands. 'When was your landlord guy out in France?' she asked.

'That's something we need to confirm.'

'And have all the handbags been attributed to a victim?'

'All except one.'

'Could that be a French victim?'

'Unless we've got another body concealed around here. And did I mention that one of the bodies was dismembered?'

'Where?'

'We don't know yet.'

'Harry, have you not been giving enough attention to your work?'

'You have been very distracting.'

'That's simply not good enough. I want to come in and see the files, and I'd like to sit in on any further interviews you do. There's someone out there who could kill again, and even if they haven't killed recently to your knowledge, there's nothing to say that they haven't killed elsewhere, or won't kill again tomorrow if the compulsion gets strong enough.'

'Chivers is already blowing his stack about the budget.'

'Then I'll come in out of the goodness of my heart. This is very dangerous territory, and you ignore the seriousness of it at your peril.'

'Stop talking and come here.'

The case was moved on, the next day. News finally came in from the brewery that the barmaid from the Covingtons' previous pub, the Robin Hood, had in fact moved on to running her own pub. A telephone call to Paula elicited the information that she must have been mistaken, so any speculation on that front had been a complete waste of time. It would seem that her husband George was just an old codger after all.

David Porter, editor of the *Carsfold Gazette*, rang in to say that his work experience youngster had turned up an advert dated just before Christmas from a 'Mike M of Castle Farthing', who had been looking for a life companion, female and under forty, so *he* wasn't let off the hook.

Timothy Driscoll, however, confirmed that the year he had spent in France covered the period in which both Annie Symons and Suzie Doidge disappeared, so that was another one off their list, provided he could come in with proof of this.

Colin Bridger and Simeon Perkins had no such confirmations of immunity to investigation so, along with Mike Mortimer, they were brought in for another round of questioning.

Each of the three suspects was shown photographs of the victims but, apart from the face of Annie Symons, all of them stated that they did not recognise the others. Unless the inspector was entirely mistaken, one of them was a very good liar – but which one?

When asked where they had been when the women were presumed to have disappeared, they were unable to answer. The times were so long ago, with no exactitude to them, and a man could hardly be expected to supply an alibi for an unspecified time in any case. When the three of them were finished with, the police were no further forward. Unlike lots of cities and larger towns, Market Darley and its surrounding villages did not boast a multitude of CCTV cameras which would help them to pick up the three men's movements through a variety of dates. In this, they were not so lucky as their urban colleagues.

When the wider team had been dismissed for the day, Falconer, Carmichael, and Tomlinson went back to their old office and the inspector summed the situation up as best as he could.

'We've got a missing young woman who hadn't disappeared at all and turned up alive and well in Spain. We've got a missing old lady who didn't fit into the pattern, and who was actually in a home and recently died of natural causes, and we've got five dead young women. With the exception of Ms Warwick's constant reminders, pokes, and prods, we had no idea whatsoever that these lonely females simply weren't around anymore.

'We've two suspects from our original five who no longer seem viable, and I've got a feeling in my water that Mr Bridger is just a distraction. He might be scared of his wife, but I somehow don't believe him capable of murder.

'That leaves us with our two gentlemen from Drovers Lane who, as Honey explained to me last night, are multi-taskers and thus capable of using diverse methods of killing – but which one might be responsible?'

This question was not to be answered that day and, apropos of nothing, Tomlinson asked if the other two were going to watch the rugby that weekend. Falconer shook his head, but Carmichael said, most unexpectedly, that he had once played for the Regional Police 2nd XV.

'Really, Sergeant? I didn't know that.'

'It was when I was a raw recruit and you didn't work here yet,' Carmichael replied. 'I'm a big bloke and so they thought I might be a bit useful to the team.'

'So why don't you play anymore?' asked Tomlinson.

'Got banned from playing for them.'

'How come?' Now Falconer was interested, too.

'Well, we didn't play rugby at our school, so I didn't know the rules, and all they told me was about passing the ball backwards, and scoring a try.'

'So what went wrong?'

'I knew about getting the ball over the line, and that's exactly what I did, but it just so happens that the ball was in our fly-half's hands as I crossed the line.'

'What?' Tomlinson couldn't quite picture it.

'The ball got caught by our fly-half, but he sort of hesitated momentarily, and I just reacted. I picked him up and raced to the line, finally grounding him and the ball.'

'You didn't, Carmichael?' Falconer was appalled.

'I did. That's why I was sent off, while the fly-half went off to have his head X-rayed, and I was eventually banned from the team.'

'You never cease to amaze me, big man,' Tomlinson chuckled.

'I'd never played the game before. How was I to know?' At the innocent look on the sergeant's face, Falconer couldn't help joining in the good-natured merriment. Carmichael held out his hands, palms up. 'What?' he asked, slightly put out by their chuckling. 'What? How was I supposed to know?'

They had needed the odd anecdote to keep them feeling cheerful, and this was certainly one about his sergeant that the inspector hadn't heard before.

Chapter Eighteen

That night Falconer had a dream. In fact, he had several, but each and every one of them ended up in front of a giant, shiny, new red front door which barred his way to anything further, and woke him up. It wasn't a menacing door, but it did seem to disrupt his dreams from progressing and he had the feeling that it was trying to impart some sort of message to him; but what would a door say? That sounded like one of Carmichael's jokes.

For the first hour or so at the station he tried to dismiss the image from his mind, but it just wouldn't shift. He began to wrack his brains to see how a giant door could be significant to his current life, but could recall no oversized doors that appeared in his everyday experience. He also didn't know of anyone with such a bright red door as this one.

When light eventually dawned, and he realised that the colour red was merely to alert his conscious mind, he made a series of phone calls: the first to Wanda Warwick. 'A gate!' he said, ending the call, and then punched in the numbers for another enquiry. 'Thank you very much, Mr Driscoll. If you do remember, will you get in touch with me?' he ended the next one. 'That's very kind of you to give me the information, Mr Bridger,' was the termination of the third call.

'Carmichael, will you print out the list that Jefferson Grammaticus sent through for me, please? I need to check it.'

'But it's a huge list, sir.'

'That's immaterial. I have to search for something on it.'

Finally, he telephoned Araminta Wingfield-Hayes in Stoney Cross, who confirmed what he had begun to suspect. His checking-up being finished, and his theory more or less confirmed, he rushed out of the meeting room, leaving everyone gaping in his wake, and immediately sought a couple of search warrants before selecting his officers. He'd also requested a man experienced in the art of detecting old blood stains invisible to the human eye.

'What's got you so fired up, sir?' asked Carmichael as they got out of the car.

'I don't want to explain in case I'm wrong, and Jelly will have my danglies for earrings,' he replied. 'But a dream I had last night might have proved to be a message from my subconscious that I simply hadn't been able to listen to before.'

'Wossat, sir?' asked the sergeant confused.

'Just do as I request, and I'll explain everything later,' he clipped. 'Tomlinson, get that door open. I expect the man's out at work. All the better for us, if we don't have him around whining. I just hope no one's seen us and we can get in and out without him being tipped off.' As he gave this instruction, he took a set of lock picks from his pocket which he had temporarily and unofficially liberated from the evidence room. 'Here, use these.'

'What are we looking for, sir?' asked Tomlinson.

'Anything that looks like a work diary. Where's the man with the blood detection equipment?'

'I'm here,' announced a deep bass voice from behind them.

'OK, do your stuff on the interior, then I want you to follow me if you don't find anything. Pay particular attention to the bathroom.'

That search ended fruitlessly, but they pressed on to the second address that Falconer needed to check. A sideboard yielded a large diary which detailed jobs for the last twelve months, now discarded in favour of one for the current year, and it didn't take long for him to find what he expected to, in an entry a year ago. It was to supply and fit a new gate for the front of Robin's Perch, Shepford St Bernard.

As the search was continuing, the unexpected arrival of Mortimer put a temporary halt to their progress – and he was in quite a temper. 'I thought we'd tidied it up pretty well,' commented Carmichael inappropriately, while Falconer made apologetic noises about having to disturb his private living quarters. He then went on to explain to him what they were looking for, and he seemed to understand the importance of them finding evidence, so he turned to go away, temporarily satisfied, and even offered to help at one point.

'Do you happen to know where Mr Perkins is

232

working at the moment?' asked Falconer.

'I think he's on that big job at Ford Hollow. You do know that he's been working away, though, don't you?'

'I had no idea,' replied the inspector. 'Can you give me any details?'

'It was somewhere in Lincoln, I think. He was going up early Monday mornings and not coming back until the Friday nights. He's only just started on the Ford Hollow development.' So, he was there when Marilyn Slade's body had been found. That must have shaken him up a bit.

'And how long was this for?'

'I think he started about the end of last spring. Why?'

'Just curiosity, Mr Mortimer,' hedged Falconer, flicking through the man's work diary again. Yes, Mortimer had been spot on. There were only a couple of references to where the site was, but he saw a few mentions of Lincoln that were more than confirmatory. 'Man-with-techy stuff, please,' he called, thinking that he really should have introduced himself properly.

'Interior, please,' he requested, and the man began to draw the curtains and spray Luminol around the room in which they were standing. Having uncovered nothing incriminating, he was directed, first to the kitchen, then upstairs. 'With special attention to the bathroom, again, if you'd be so kind.'

'You're too polite for your own good,' commented Tomlinson, but Falconer was too busy staring out of the kitchen window. There was a fair-sized shed at the bottom of the narrow garden, and he was suddenly desperate to have a look inside it.

'Nothing up here,' declared the man with the spray as he trotted down the stairs, and the inspector explained about the wooden structure outside. Leading the way, Falconer almost ran towards the outbuilding, only to be temporarily thwarted by the large padlock that secured the door.

'Carmichael, heavy metal implement, if you would be so kind.'

'They'll all be in the shed, won't they, sir?'

Tomlinson had headed off, however, and returned a couple of minutes later with a crowbar. 'In the cupboard under the stairs,' he stated by way of explanation, and the inspector used it to prise off the clasp that held the padlock secure.

As he threw open the door he thought he must be wrong. There were no visible signs of a body having been dismembered in its interior. In fact, the whole interior was coated in a dark creosote-like substance and the concrete floor looked spotless. Oh God, maybe he had been wrong after all. He felt a great wave of failure and foolishness wash over him until the man with the spray asked them to leave while he covered the window. When he'd done his stuff and reopened the door, there was all the evidence they needed to make an arrest.

When they had all squashed inside to witness it, he sprayed again, and almost the whole of the floor showed traces, glowing blue in the semi-darkness, of having had blood splashed about liberally. Although a dead body might not spurt arterial blood, it certainly gave off a lot of the red stuff if it was cut up, and this was clearly where Bonnie Fletcher had been dismembered. Further forensic tests would prove it. 'And I suppose no one would think anything was wrong if they heard a handyman using an electric saw in his shed. No neighbour would suspect anything. They'd just think he was making something,' the inspector whispered, almost to himself.

'These walls look newly painted,' said the techy, 'we'll bring in the new infra-red camera which can detect blood traces through several layers of paint.'

Tomlinson had temporarily wandered off, but he now came racing down the garden waving his arms. 'Perkins is back,' he hissed.

'Great,' said Falconer, 'At least we don't have to go find him. Are there any cuffs in the car?' he asked, as they were not in his inconvenient two-seater.

'There are indeed. I made sure of it before we left.' Tomlinson was turning into a very satis-factory officer.

'Right, Tomlinson, to the car to get them. I'll go back and cover the rear, you, Carmichael, go to the front door and get his attention. We'll have him in custody between us.'

The three men separated, and in a short time they had their bird in handcuffs. He had sub-mitted with only token resistance, as if he had known the game was up. Granted, he had sub-mitted while yelling for a solicitor, and with a little light persuasion from the sergeant, but it wasn't long before they had him back in Market Darley police station, booked in by the custody officer and waiting in a cell.

'But how did you know it was him, sir?' asked Carmichael, when the man was safely locked away. 'I mean, apart from the presence of blood. How did you know to go there?'

'Telephone,' one of the DCs called across the office.

Slightly annoyed at his big moment being interrupted, the inspector took the handset and found Timothy Driscoll on the other end of the call.

'You told me to get in touch if I remembered who did those estimates for me,' he stated. 'I've actually come across them in a box of papers I brought back with me. Do you want me to bring them in?'

'Who were they submitted by?'

'A bloke called Perkins – general building and decorating work undertaken, according to this paperwork.'

'I'll get someone right over to collect them. Thank you, Mr Driscoll, for taking the time to find them.'

'The box needed sorting through. You gave me the extra push. It's a lot better than being a suspect in a multiple murder case.'

'You're right there, sir. And in any case, as you weren't in England when the first two women disappeared, we didn't seriously consider you,' replied Falconer, his fingers crossed behind his back because, of course, they had done. 'I'll dispatch an officer straight away to collect those estimates from you.'

'What was that all about?' asked Carmichael.

'Just another piece of the jigsaw falling into

place. Anyway, I'll have to go and interview Mr Perkins, as I'm quite sure his solicitor will have arrived by now. Carmichael, you come in with me. Tomlinson, you can stand duty at the door. That way you'll hear a lot of the story, then I can return here to apprise the whole team of the outcome of these murders.'

Chapter Nineteen

In the interview room, Falconer faced his opponent. After starting the tapes and confirming the date and the names of those present, he began the questioning.

'Can you confirm that you carried out estimates for refurbishment of flats at number seven King George III Terrace in Stoney Cross in spring 2009?'

'Can't remember; I do a lot of jobs.'

'Did you meet any of the occupants of those flats?'

'Don't remember.'

'Did you then go on to strangle a woman living in one of those flats, by the name of Suzie Doidge, and dump her body in a ditch in the vicinity of Market Darley on or after 10th April 2009?'

'This is outrageous, Inspector. Surely this is not an approved interviewing tactic,' stated the solicitor.

'No comment.'

'Mr Perkins, can you confirm that you carried

out the redecoration of the cottage next door to your own, number two Drovers Lane, Castle Farthing? You will remember that you denied that you knew the tenant, Annie Symons, in a previous interview.'

'No comment,' replied Perkins.

'I really must object to this form of questioning. Nothing has been proved against my client.'

'Did you then go on to kill the tenant, Annie Symons, stabbing her with a blade, and concealing her body in the woods to the south of Castle Farthing on or after 17th May 2009?'

'No comment.'

'Did you hang and fit a new front door at number six Prince Albert Terrace, in Steynham St Michael, in January 2010?'

'No comment.'

'And did you go on to kill the occupant of said property, Marilyn Slade, by stabbing her, and then burying her body in a shallow grave, on wasteland near the ford on the outskirts of Ford Hollow during or after January 2010?'

'No comment.'

'I shall be making a formal complaint about your questioning technique, Inspector Falconer,' interjected the solicitor.

'Did you carry out duties in regard to the refurbishment of a country hotel known as The Manse, near Carsfold, in the late spring of 2010?'

'No comment.'

'And did you go on to conceal the body of a young woman by the name of Melanie Saunders, whom you had killed by cutting her throat, at said hotel, beside the recently turned-over land on which the new driveway was laid, sometime in May of 2010?'

'Utterly outrageous and untenable.' The solicitor was trying his hardest to throw Falconer, but he hadn't exactly got up and left, or insisted that the interview be terminated.

'No comment.' This was said in the voice of a man not quite so sure of himself. Perkins' solicitor gave him a sideways glance, his face a mask of dawning defeat.

'Did you hang a new front gate at Robin's Perch in Shepford St Bernard for a Miss Bonnie Fletcher?'

'No comment.'

'And did you then kill Miss Fletcher, the owner of the aforementioned property, dismember her body in the garden shed at your home, number three Drovers Lane in Castle Farthing, and dispose of the body parts in the septic tank while you were re-laying some of the drains at a house known as The Mill, in Stoney Cross, during February 2011?'

'I think I need a private word with my client, if you'd be so good.'

Perkins sat in absolute silence after this last question, and refused to utter another word for the rest of the time the three detectives were in the room, and totally ignored his legal representative.

'I should like a little time to consult with my client,' requested the stunned solicitor once more, and the interview was formally concluded.

As Perkins, together with his solicitor, was led back to his cell to undertake the interview that the man's legal representative so needed to have with his client, Falconer and his two colleagues returned to the rest of the team in the large room that they now considered their home office for the duration of this investigation.

Calling for silence, he addressed all the officers who had assisted him with computer work and house-to-house enquiries, but before he could begin his explanation of how light had dawned on him of the probable culprit, a young DC at the back of the room shot to his feet, a hand in the air like an eager schoolboy. 'Sir, sir,' he exclaimed, 'I've finally located that cousin in Australia!' he yelled, a look of triumph on his face.

With the slightest of smirks on his face, Falconer said, 'How very satisfying for you, Constable.' This was his show time and he'd run it his way.

'I had a dream last night,' he announced self-importantly, 'about a giant red door, and I had no idea what it meant.' A sea of quizzical faces turned towards him at this strange remark. 'It recurred in so many of my dreams that I realised it must mean something. When it came to me, it was stunningly obvious what my mind had picked up without informing the conscious me.

'On this investigation, we had come across a door that had been the latest piece of work done on the property in Prince Albert Terrace. This front door was only a couple of years old, whereas the window frames and the general state of repair on the outside of the house indicated that this had been a piece of work carried out on its own, and it got me thinking.

'I'd been desperate to find a link between all these dead women. Just as an aside, I did at one

240

point wonder if it might be the lonely hearts column of the *Carsfold Gazette*, but a couple of chats with the editor soon put me off that tack. Now, my mind also dredged up the unappreciated fact that Annie Symon's cottage had just been redecorated before she disappeared.

'We didn't really make enough of the fact that Mortimer and Perkins could turn their hands to just about anything. It was only earlier today that I confirmed by telephone with Mr Bridger, the owner of the Drovers Lane property, that Perkins had done the decorating, even though he'd never volunteered this information or even admitted to having been in the house, let alone having known Ms Symons.

'It had also come to our notice that Mr Driscoll had estimates done for the refurbishment of the King George III Terrace property. As luck would have it, after we had established that he couldn't have committed the first two murders, he was rummaging through a box of sundries that he had brought back from France, when he happened to come across the estimates sent to him while he was out of England on his European adventure. What an act of serendipitous synchronicity that was for us. The estimates were done by Simeon Perkins.

'Mr Jefferson Grammaticus, the owner of The Manse, sent a list of all the works done for the conversion of the country house into an hotel, and I was able to ascertain that Mr Perkins was working at the place both before and after the un-executed job interview Mr Grammaticus had scheduled with Melanie Saunders. It wouldn't have been hard for him to conceal himself on the property, or in the unsecured woods behind it, and drag in a body that needed disposing of, to the recently turned soil waiting for its topcoat of the drive.

'So far, so good. Now we come to Bonnie Fletcher, whose disappearance from her home in Shepford St Bernard was the only one initially reported to us, and whom we didn't realise was part of this killing spree. Miss Wingfield-Hayes, in whose septic tank Fletcher's body parts were found, had had some work done on a partially collapsed drain pipe at about the time that the woman went missing. The workman was Simeon Perkins.

'We now believe that he dismembered her body in his garden shed and disposed of the parts during his works at Stoney Cross. Forensics is gathering evidence not only from his shed but from his van. Miss Wingfield-Hayes has confirmed that she stayed with a friend locally while she was unable to use her sanitary facilities, and so Perkins would have had easy unhindered access to the tank.

'Poor Suzie Doidge, that most difficult to locate lady, had had her body unceremoniously dumped in a ditch in a remote part of some farming land.'

'When I put together the information that we already had, scant though it was, and made a few phone calls to confirm what I already suspected, I was proved right. I just needed to eliminate the other builder, Mike Mortimer, as they worked together sometimes. No need to cheer, lads,' he said, giving a little bow. 'But it was the only connection that could be established between all our victims.'

'We just have to hope, now that Simeon Perkins knows that he's been rumbled, without knowledge of the amount of solid evidence we've got, that he cracks and confesses all to his solicitor, then signs a full confession. I think I rattled him during our very one-sided "no comment" interview, during which his solicitor went from purple with rage to white with shock.

'We've got him until tomorrow afternoon, anyway, and I want to set something up for the morning. I'm going to bring in someone who might be able to work on him from a psychological point of view.' This produced not only a slight smile from him, but also from Carmichael.

'It'll be nice to see Dr Dubois again,' the sergeant commented, seemingly in innocence.

Tomlinson took his cue like a professional. 'Do you think you could get her to bring in a punnet of cherries? I heard that she was very fond of them, and I quite fancy some too.'

Carmichael held his breath at such outrageous cheek but Falconer, unexpectedly, took this remark very well and cocked an eyebrow at the younger man. He knew when someone was trying to get a rise out of him.

'I hear they're in very short supply round here, Constable. I doubt she'll be able to find even one,' and, whistling to himself, he left the office to head for the canteen.

That evening he discussed the surprising developments of the day with Honey, who had come round to see how the case was going. She could have phoned, of course, but that wouldn't have given her the opportunity to lead him by the hand back to their special spot in paradise which, in her mind, was right in the middle of his bed.

After an omelette and salad, he explained his very busy day and how the questioning of their suspect – definitely the murderer – had gone. 'What really twists my guts,' he said, 'is why? Why did he kill any of them – and I don't somehow think he's going to tell me. I wondered if you'd have a talk with him. Of course, Chivers won't possibly agree to add your services to his budget...'

'No worries. I'll do this one as a personal favour to you, free, gratis, and on the house. This guy obviously has a severe mental problem and, from what you've told me about him, I consider him to be a serious risk to women, and think that he'll kill again, for what that's worth.'

'Trouble is, he's quite a good-looking man, and I can see vulnerable women being easily charmed by him. If we can obtain anymore proof that it was him, through further enquiries, I should be able to get the CPS to take us seriously. I want this man locked away, there's no doubt in my mind that he's guilty.'

'Maybe having me serve his crimes up to him as one giant course might move him to confront the totality of what he's done. I think getting him to tell me why he committed the murders might also make things more real for him. The telling might inspire some emotional reaction.'

'Glass of wine?' asked Falconer, rising from his seat.

'I'm terribly tired, actually,' replied Honey, faking a yawn. 'I think maybe we could do with an early night.'

'By George, I think you're right,' replied the inspector, grinning with anticipation. No doubt the gilt would wear off the gingerbread with time but, for now, it was completely golden in his eyes.

Chapter Twenty

When Falconer and Honey walked into the temporary CID office together the next morning, there was a chorus of wolf whistles and ribald comments. 'Behave yourselves!' he barked in his usual tones, and faces fell, before his face split in a grin of delight at this approval from his team.

'I'm sorry I didn't bring any cherries with me,' Honey said in a carrying voice, 'but Harry here is all out of them.' Tomlinson had the grace to blush. His boss was not like other men, who slept around on a casual basis, and he was glad he had not been considered to be crossing a line with his impertinent jokey comment of the day before. By God, but Dr Honey Dubois was a truly beautiful woman – and, if he was honest, Falconer wasn't such a bad catch either. They made a handsome couple.

'OK, listen up, everybody! This is the mental health expert I want to consult with regard to our Mr Perkins, and I'm going to get Dr Dubois to interview him with a female member of staff present. She has confided to me that there might be some things that our suspect might not be happy to talk about in the presence of other men.

245

'When she's finished her interview we can listen to the tape afterwards, if she manages to get to him. I'm just going with her now to arrange for the man himself to be brought to an interview room and summon a female officer. I'll be back shortly.'

He was a man of his word, but Honey did not return for hours, and when she did, she looked quite harrowed.

'Did he talk about his motives? Did he even own up to what he'd done?' asked the inspector, assuming that she hadn't been battering her head against a brick wall all this time.

'Yes and yes,' she said with a sad smile. 'And I definitely think he's a public danger, even though he returned to his cell in tears. I think the truth of his actions has finally hit him, and your questioning yesterday,' here she nodded at Falconer, 'has made him acknowledge that it wasn't just recreational or a game. They were real women, and not his playthings.'

'Sit down and tell us,' urged Falconer. 'We've all worked on this case, and we could do with knowing what we were up against.'

'I'll just give you a quick run-down,' she replied. 'As with so many murders of this kind, it was all tied up with sex. When he asked Suzie Doidge' – she consulted her brief notes for the name of the first victim – 'out for a drink, he had no plans to hurt her, but he was rather hoping that she might put out on a first date. He had gathered that she was a lady of, shall we say, easy virtue, and he'd not had a partner for some time. I suppose you guys,' she said with a twinkle, 'after the welcome

246

you gave Harry and I, would say that he was gagging for it.' Here, she paused to an embarrassed silence.

'The man had actually put a mattress in the back of his van. After he'd plied Suzie with alcohol, he didn't drive her straight home, but took her to a secluded spot and enticed her into the back of the van. Apparently she was quite willing, but the man lost his erection before he could enter her, and she made the, in this case fatal, mistake of laughing. She was quite drunk.

'When he couldn't recapture the moment, and she carried on laughing, he said he just saw red and, in frustration, grabbed the first thing to hand, which happened to be a knife that he had in the van with a load of other tools. He stated that the next thing he knew, she was dead. He had to dump the body somewhere, and when he'd done that, in horror, he returned home and burnt the clothes on which he had sustained bloodstains and cleaned the inside of his van with bleach.'

'And was that the pattern for all the murders?'

'No, not really. But he found he couldn't achieve an erection at all without the thought of violence, and he began to vent his sexual frustration with violence culminating in murder.

'It's probably best that the bodies weren't in good condition, because he had to cause some injury when the women weren't willing, but the sexual urge is very strong in some, and overcomes everything else. If it weren't for the fact that the thought of killing them was his particular trigger, we would probably still be dealing with a series of rapes.'

'It's all on the tape, if you want to listen to it. If you don't mind, though, I'd rather not go through it again quite so soon. I will tell you about the trophies, however. When he'd dumped Suzie Doidge's body and got home he found he'd still got her handbag in the passenger seat-well of his van, and whenever he looked at it thereafter, he was able to relive his experience. When that wore off, he killed again.

'When you found the first body, he panicked because he had all the handbags in his spare bed-room and took them off to some waste ground and buried them. By the way, you'll find the handbag belonging to a Lincolnshire woman in along with the ones you found. You'll have to pass that evidence on to the relevant police authority, but it looks like there's a sixth victim buried on wasteland up there.

'Do you think I could go get a coffee now? It was rather a sickening experience, even given my background with mental health problems.'

'Thank you so much for your time, Dr Dubois,' Falconer said. 'I'll have to get your interview cleared by Chivers to submit it as evidence, but if I tell him that you came in of your own accord without promise of a fee, perhaps he'll relent and make you a payment for professional services, especially if it wraps up five murders.'

'I really don't care after what I've just listened to. That man needs taking off the streets, and I should advise you to put out a warning to all women to be careful whom they employ to carry out repair or maintenance works on their homes, if they're on their own. I'm going to get that

248

coffee, then go home for a shower. I feel soiled.'

Perkins signed a statement of confession that afternoon, and Falconer went to see the superintendent, to keep him up to date. It would appear that the good news had preceded his visit, for he found the superior officer in a very good mood, anticipating the glory that would, no doubt, be heaped on his head. So happy was he that he would not have to keep on the extra DCs any longer, or allow any more of his precious budget on the case, that he agreed to make the minimum payment to Dr Dubois and confirm that she had been employed professionally for her services.

'Good work, Inspector. It may have cost a packet to solve this one, but at least it's not going to cost anymore on investigation. I know we've used Dr Dubois' services before, but I'd forgotten exactly how good she was. Tell your team well done from me. Now, get on with whatever you do in that office of yours.'

He really didn't remember what it had been like to be actively involved in an investigation, thought Falconer, as he went back downstairs to the office to tell the extra men they could now return to their home forces. It would just be the three of them again: him, Carmichael, and Tomlinson. He'd be quite relieved to see the status quo return.

His sergeant nipped out of the station at lunchtime to visit his wife, and came back for the afternoon looking absolutely delighted. 'Guess what, sir?' he asked, as he picked up one of the chairs that would have to be returned to the corridor.

'What, Carmichael?'

'Kerry and the twins are coming home later

today and I can send my mum back home.'

'Congratulations.'

'And,' continued the very happy man, 'I won't have to put my slippers on at the door when I get in, or fold my newspaper and put it in the recycling box every night.'

As it was just common sense to Falconer to follow these guidelines, he merely nodded in agreement, not quite understanding why his sergeant was so pleased at returning to what were obviously rather lax practices.

With the crime clear-up rate considerably improved for the month, if not the year, the inspector left the station a happy man that night, but was very surprised to find Honey waiting for him by his car, having already phoned him to see what time he was leaving.

'Is something wrong?' he asked, with a sinking feeling in the pit of his stomach.

'Harry, I need to ask you something,' she said in a voice full of trepidation.

'What?'

'Will you marry me?'

Detective Inspector Harry Falconer stood in the Market Darley police station car park, beside his Boxster, with his mouth wide open, so surprised he couldn't speak.

The publishers hope that this book has given you enjoyable reading. Large Print Books are especially designed to be as easy to see and hold as possible. If you wish a complete list of our books please ask at your local library or write directly to:

Magna Large Print Books
Magna House, Long Preston,
Skipton, North Yorkshire.
BD23 4ND

This Large Print Book for the partially sighted, who cannot read normal print, is published under the auspices of

THE ULVERSCROFT FOUNDATION